THE FALCON CHRONICLES: BOOK TWO

GHOSTS
OF THE
FOREST

Also by Steve Backshall

Tiger Wars
Wilds of the Wolf (coming in 2014)

THE FALCON CHRONICLES: BOOK TWO

GHOSTS
OF THE
FOREST

STEVE BACKSHALL

Orion
Children's Books

First published in Great Britain in 2013
by Orion Children's Books
a division of the Orion Publishing Group Ltd
Orion House
5 Upper St Martin's Lane
London WC2H 9EA
An Hachette UK Company

1 3 5 7 9 10 8 6 4 2

ISBN 978 1 4440 0439 7

Printed in Great Britain by Clays Ltd, St Ives plc

www.orionbooks.co.uk

To my editor, Fiona, and mentor, Julian.
For good advice and guidance with the lightest
of touches. Thank you. SB.

Only after the last tree has been cut down.
Only after the last river has been poisoned.
Only after the last fish has been caught.
Only then will you find that money cannot be eaten.

Cree Indian Prophecy

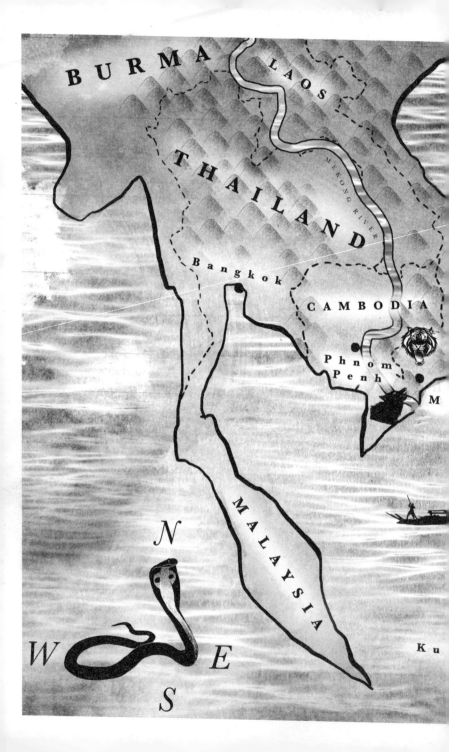

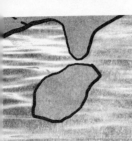

GHOSTS
OF THE
FOREST

Another adventure begins ...

VIETNAM

Ho Chi
inh City

SOUTH CHINA SEA

Kota
Kinabalu

Brunei

Mulu
Mountains

ching

BORNEO

 Sinter

 The Clan

 Saker

PROLOGUE

The fat man adjusted his belt, opening it one more notch. Any further, and he would have to cut down on the noodles. Either that or buy a new belt. He breathed a little more easily, placed his coffee on the desk, adjusted his 500-dollar silk tie and twisted around on his green leather swivel chair. Before him, the vast window of his office stared out onto a sumptuous lagoon, its pontoons lined with super-yachts. The lagoon was man-made; just five years ago the area had been twisted mangroves, full of birds, crocodiles and monkeys. Sharks and other sea beasts made their nurseries among the tangled roots of the submerged mangrove trees. Now it was a marina bustling with the elite of modern Borneo. The swanky office block was the centrepiece of the development, and Amir's office was the penthouse. The building housed both the Malaysian environmental agency, and their logging headquarters. Amir was the president of both. Despite the outrage of conservation organisations, the man whose job it was to protect the rainforests of Southeast Asia also gained the most from cutting them down.

Amir didn't have a problem with that. To him it was all about making the most of Malaysia's resources. Places like Britain and Australia had cut down all their forests; who were they to say Malaysia should not do the same? Of course, if he got very, very rich from it, then that would be even better.

It had been a very good week for Amir's bank accounts. Several logging companies were bidding for the right to cut down big chunks of forest. They were going to turn them into palm oil and acacia plantations. Each contract contained a kickback for Amir, and he'd already bought a luxurious house in America and another on the harbour in Sydney. His wasn't the biggest yacht in the marina in front of him, but he was working on that.

Life was pretty good, but it was not perfect. He'd been hit by a flour bomb at the Malaysian parliament a few weeks ago. It had been thrown by some greenie lunatic. He'd also had death threats from crazed environmental groups, none of which he took seriously. He'd made front-page news in the *Straits Times* talking about the "enviromentals" or "bunny huggers", and about how Malaysia would be a global superpower within a decade, by exploiting the "living gold" of the forests of Borneo.

Today however, something had happened that made his skin clammy with fear.

Amir had come to work that morning as he did every day, greeted his secretary, walked into his plush office and dropped his briefcase. Then in his regular ritual, he went to get himself a coffee, which he placed on his leather-clad desk. He set to reading his mail, perfectly arranged on his desk with crisply ironed copies of the *Financial Times* and the *Wall Street Journal*. However, something on top of the mail caught his attention. It was a carving about the size of his thumb, made from a piece of fine rainforest wood. He knew instantly from the weight, the espresso coffee colour and swirly grain that this was a rare tropical ironwood. A whole tree could be worth 20,000 dollars, more than everyone combined in a native village might earn in a year. He picked it up, admiring the beautiful grain and the smoothness of the unvarnished carving. Someone had spent hours making this, and taken great care over it. But why would anyone send him a wooden bullet?

Amir reached across to the intercom on his desk; "Ibu, come in here please." Within seconds, his secretary was in the office, pad poised.

"Ibu, who sent me this?" he demanded, proffering the bullet between finger and thumb.

"I have no idea, Bapak," she responded. "Was it among your letters?"

"No, you know it wasn't; it was here on top of my newspapers!" Amir laughed; surely it was part of some game by one of his colleagues. His secretary shook her head.

"No, Bapak, I put those papers there just a minute ago, and there was nothing else here." Something told him she was telling the truth.

Amir paused, then ushered her out. Alone, he wondered what this could mean. The building had a high-tech surveillance system, armed police, and security cameras everywhere. No one could stroll in, place a wooden bullet on his desk and then just walk out again. How could this have happened? As he pondered, he looked at his newspaper. On top lay a piece of paper with a message. It read:

> *Your actions are destroying the forests the whole planet depends on. We are watching and do not forgive. We are going to take from you everything you value.*

It was signed, *The Ghosts of the Forest.* At first he snorted with derisive laughter. But something about it troubled him. Whoever had walked right into his well-guarded office and placed a bullet on his desk could as easily have placed a real bullet in his skull. It was a well-chosen warning. He pursed his lips, and his brow furrowed. He turned the carved wooden trinket in his fingers. On the underside, where the firing cap would be in a real bullet, was a symbol. Burned into the wood like a brand was the simple outline of a bird of prey. The brooding head of a Saker falcon.

1

Saker started, his heart pounding, his senses on high alert. A demonic screech cut the air, like the scream of a child in terrible pain. Nearby, an explosion of feathers from the frantic wing beats of fruit doves panicked from their slumber. Every one of Saker's muscles tightened, preparing to leap into flight, yet the faces close to him in the shadows didn't flinch. He forced himself to relax; the noise must surely have been the call of some forest bird, one of the thousands he had yet to learn. Telling himself to chill out, he closed his eyes and drew in a deep, calming breath. The air was so thick with moisture he could taste it. Scents of distant fruiting fig and tamarind were sticky in his nostrils. Above, a full moon was occasionally visible through the tangled tendrils of the jungle canopy. Shafts of white moonlight penetrated the heavy air. It was so bright that it was as if someone had dropped a car out of the sky, and it had found its final resting place up in the treetops, its headlights glaring down on the forest floor. The hunters beneath, perhaps ten of them, stepped around the pools of light, hugging tight to the shadows.

Saker was dressed in the same way as his silent companions; a loincloth around his waist, twisted leather and palm bracelets circling his upper arm and ankles. Dark smears of plant dye across his cheeks and chest served to break up his outline like the nebulous stripes and spots of a clouded leopard, helping him to become one with the night. Around his throat was a wooden amulet carved in the shape of a crocodile. All moved barefoot, toes gently feeling for brittle twigs and dry leaves that might betray a careless step with a crackle or rustle. Each man carried in his hand a three metre long blowpipe called a *keleput*, cut from a single length of wood and hollowed out with a bone drill. Using this, they could propel a poisoned dart perhaps twenty metres with lethal accuracy. The darts were little more than flimsy toothpicks, carved from the stems of palm fronds, but coated in toxins gathered from the sticky latex of the *tajem* tree. They could kill a monkey in seconds, or stop a man's heart in minutes.

Another odd sound. This time not so blood-curdling. The men in the shadows stiffened, their senses keen. The sound came again: it was the chirrup of a bush cricket's wings rubbing together. Saker knew it was a signal made by the practised lips of the tribe's front tracker, telling them, "Stop, listen, there is danger ahead." Saker squinted,

6

trying to make sense of the darkness. His eyes were already accustomed to the night, but it seemed the tribesmen around him were much more capable, their nocturnal vision like a forest cat's. They could clearly see something he couldn't. After a few seconds' concentration, what he thought were distant fireflies became weak electric lights; it was a camp. Civilisation! His fingers brushed the wooden handle of the long *tueh* knife at his hip. His companions had been quiet before, but now they became ghosts of the forest, no more than a memory as they stole through the night.

Abruptly the caverns of the forest came to an end, and before them lay a smouldering field. It was peppered by the sad stumps of ancient ironwood trees; deep furrows showed where clunking yellow machines had dragged away trees that had been growing for centuries. The timber was bound for Malaysian logging mills to make wood chips to line suburban flower borders and rabbit hutches. The logging camp in the centre of the wasteland had been built to last no more than a few weeks. That was all it would take to totally eradicate this patch of forest that had been here for tens of thousands of years.

The camp was centred around two cabins and a ragtag collection of flapping blue tarpaulins. Campfires crackled, and mangy-looking dogs, chickens and a few flea-bitten pigs picked around piles of rubbish in search of scraps. A scratchy stereo blasted out a whining voice, a crude copy of a Western pop song. Saker winced; it sounded as if the singer had been sucking on a helium balloon, and the backing track seemed to have been played on a ten-dollar synthesiser. It couldn't have been more out of place against the glorious cicada, frog and cricket orchestra that was the natural soundtrack of the Bornean jungle night.

On the other side of the clearing several vehicles were rusting in the mud – huge, battered Toyota Land Cruisers with tyres as tall as a man. There was an industrial digger, and trucks loaded with felled trees as grand in scale and size as the columns on the Parthenon. Each tree was daubed with paint showing where it was felled and where it would be sent. The trunks were four metres in diameter. Saker glanced at one of his companions waiting for the next signal. In the white moonlight, he noticed the trickle of a tear running down the man's cheek. The man looked back at Saker, aware of his gaze. The tribesman made a series of gestures, pointing to the clearing with his thumb, looking up at the sky. Then, taking the amulet around his neck, he rubbed it, and closed his eyes. This place was sacred. It had been a grove where his ancestors had been buried over the centuries. It was one of the last places the treasured ironwood trees had been preserved from the loggers' chainsaws. His forefathers' spirits were one with the living wood. Those trees were now stacked on a truck and bound for the sawmill.

His people, the Penan, kept no photographs or mementos. They believed that the dead would always live in the forest, watching over their descendants like guardian angels. This was more than a vandalised graveyard. It was as if the outsiders had murdered his family.

Saker felt his muscles tensing again. Without him realising it, his teeth clenched and adrenalin started to leak into his blood, quickening his heart rate. The Clan, who had been Saker's family, called this sensation "the rush", the moment of excitement before a kill, when wolves yip and whine with bloodlust, and an assassin's fingertips tingle. They were taught that when they felt the rush, they should breathe deep to quell the adrenalin. Those who didn't might unleash a spear too early, or make rash decisions. The Penan as hunters knew the rush just as well, and doubtless had their own name for it. They had to be cautious. They'd been doing whatever they could to sabotage this plunder of their lands for over a decade now, and the loggers would be ready. They'd be armed with shotguns and possibly even automatic rifles. Anyone who was captured would be shot. Now was not the time to stampede in with a wasted war cry.

They split, moving around the outskirts of the clearing, heading for the monstrous vehicles. Their bare feet squelched in the orange mud – all that remained now that the fragile jungle top soils had been exposed. A tall man had stepped out of the cabin and into the pool of light beneath an occasionally flickering naked lightbulb. He was no more than three steps from Saker. Saker pursed his lips, making the bush cricket chirp that meant, "stop, pay attention". The logger's features were briefly illuminated, and Saker smelled the acidic phosphorous from a struck match. The man had pockmarked swarthy cheeks – scarring from teenage acne – and a wispy moustache. As he breathed out a cloud of perfumed smoke from his *kretek* cigarette, Saker's nostrils registered the sweet smell of cloves. He could have reached over and plunged his knife up to the hilt in the man's chest, but this was against the ways of the peaceful Penan. Saker knew that if he did anything violent, he would wake up alone in the forest tomorrow. His companions would have gone, leaving not so much as a footprint to prove they had ever existed.

Saker merged into the background, swaying imperceptibly in the gentle wind like a praying mantis, to mimic the slight movement of the trees. Saker's eyes were already adjusted to the darkness, pupils wide to absorb as much light as possible, while the man had just stepped out of the artificial light, leaving him with no night vision. Saker was as good as invisible to him. The logger sucked the last of his cigarette and dropped the stub, crushing it under the heel of his cowboy boot. He turned, and walked back inside.

With the threat gone, the Penan glided through the camp, intent on quiet destruction. Petrol caps were untwisted, and sugar poured into the fuel tanks. Tyres were slashed and fan belts sliced. The chainsaws that bit so cruelly into the flesh of the sacred trees had their chainlinks sprung and starting cords cut. The larger machines that could deal out the most deadly terror on the forest received special attention. The Penan had seen their first motor vehicles less than a decade before, but had quickly learned how best to paralyse them.

No matter how satisfying it was to see hydraulic fluid spilling into the mud, or to pull out electric wires, the Penan knew their actions were ultimately useless. The loggers had the Malaysian government behind them. They might stop the diggers rolling for a few days, but parts would soon be shipped, and the chainsaws would rage again. All it would take would be one satellite phone call . . . Saker's attention was caught by a long aerial sticking up out of one of the cabins. It was a radio antenna. Almost all of these logging camps had portable satellite dishes that enabled them to keep in touch with the outside world, but the dense ceiling of forest often cut out the signal. This camp was relying on old-fashioned radio technology! If Saker could sabotage that system, the loggers would have to walk to the nearest town, and that might take two or three days. It would certainly slow their recovery. Saker crept across the mud towards the light. There was an urgent snort from behind him, the alarm call of a proboscis monkey made by one of the Penan, trying to catch his attention. Saker knew the message behind the sound: "You're straying from the plan! Don't do anything stupid!" He didn't even glance back.

The aerial was on top of one of the makeshift buildings. Saker climbed up using the windowsills as footholds, and slid over the roof. He moved with great caution, aware that the plastic ceiling was taut as a drum, and footfalls would sound like a boom to the people inside. The aerial was attached to a large black box, to keep the workings safe from jungle rain. Saker used the tip of his knife to unscrew one side of the box and pull it away. Inside was a morass of wires he didn't know how to operate, but did know how to sabotage. He reached inside, grabbed a handful, and pulled.

It was as if he had grabbed hold of an electric cow fence with both hands. The shock threw him bodily backwards onto the roof with an involuntary shriek. He rolled straight to his feet, prepared to leap off the roof and run. Instantly a commotion started inside, and within seconds he found himself staring down into blinding torchlight. This time the tables were turned; it was the logger who had light on his side. The man shouted at him in a language Saker didn't understand. Behind the glare of the torch, Saker could just make out the sheen of a gun-barrel. He slid down and dropped to the mud.

The whole mission had been compromised because of him. The Penan would have melted into the forest by now, and he might never find them again.

The pockmarked man gesticulated with the rifle, barking questions Saker couldn't understand. Saker's mind screamed, searching for a way out. He certainly couldn't count on mercy. These were lawless, hard men. Unless Saker found a way out, they would kill him and dump his body where it would never be found.

The loggers couldn't comprehend why anyone would want to live in the forest. For them it was hot, wet, humid, thick with biting bugs, a miserable hell that made all their equipment and clothing rust and rot. But they hadn't seen the wonders that Saker had: hidden waterfalls hung with hundred-year-old pepper vines, the haunting songs of gibbons echoing over a misty valley as the sun began to rise. And most of all, they knew nothing of the orang utan, the old man of the forest. To Saker and the Penan, it was a totem animal. Our own image, clothed in umber fur, tranquilly munching fruit in the treetops. The forests had to remain, or the orang utan would fade away, and take with it a big part of our souls. It was the orangs that had drawn Saker to Borneo. He hoped that he might be able to do something to help the forests, to help the apes. But the loggers were city folk, hated the forest, and cared nothing for the orang utan. Furthermore, as they were getting paid per tree they cut down, the efforts of the saboteurs took money from their pockets.

As his mind raced, his eye was caught by the glimmer of naked metal behind the shoulder of his adversary. It was one of the Penan – he'd come back! It was Leysin, the man he had seen shedding a tear earlier. His long *tueh* knife was drawn, and it was clear he intended to plunge it into the back of the logger. Saker couldn't let that happen. Penan culture had no truck with killers; Leysin would be made an outcast. Saker raised his hands in the universal gesture of surrender, then stepped towards his captor.

The pockmarked man raised the rifle from his hip to his shoulder, clearly telling Saker to stay exactly where he was. The boy nodded, and spoke in a placating voice, "I'm really sorry man, I just have friends who live here, that's all." It didn't matter what he said; he was just buying time. "Come on, you don't want to waste bullets on me!"

Leysin crept forward, knife held high. Saker had to act. He snapped his hand out and grabbed the tip of the rifle barrel, pulling it towards himself, then rolling his whole body in a balletic move down the length of the gun towards the Malaysian. When his back lay flat against the gun, Saker jacked his elbow into the throat of his captor, who doubled up, gasping for breath. Saker then took his legs from under him with a leg sweep, like a farmer reaping corn with a scythe. The rifle and its owner dropped unceremoniously into the mud. Saker and Leysin ran for the shadows.

As they scampered over the exposed roots and tree stumps, shouting rang out, and then several cracks, and the whiz of bullets about their ears. It was panic fire; the loggers couldn't see them in the darkness and were shooting blindly. Almost at the trees, Saker ducked as another round fizzed overhead. Then the welcoming arms of the jungle cloaked him in its dark blanket. But he was alone. Where was Leysin? Squinting back towards the bedlam of the camp, Saker made out a shadowy figure struggling to get up from the dirt. Saker turned and ran back towards him. Torch beams sliced the darkness, but the loggers were scared to venture into the jungle at night. Saker grabbed the Penan, who lay breathing heavily, and dragged him towards safety, as more shots rang out and angry voices screamed vengeance. Leysin could still keep himself upright, but only just. Saker propelled him forwards, taking one arm over his shoulder and putting his hand round Leysin's waist. He could feel warm sticky blood around Leysin's midriff; at least one of the bullets had found its mark. They stumbled off, the Penan hunter groaning with every step.

2

The scent of something putrid in the gutter teased Sinter's nostrils, making her shudder. She told herself not to look. No good ever came of looking. One bloated dog corpse looked just the same as any other, and who knows, it could be something worse. About her, the throng of humanity seethed like termites labouring to rebuild a damaged nest. Along the narrow alleys street vendors had set up small stalls selling fruits and vegetables. Some of the fruit looked like absurd children's toys, purple, scarlet, and covered with lumps, bumps and spikes; others she had never seen before. There were bundles of coloured cloths, pirated DVDs, and wicker platters filled with volcanoes of spice and herbs. Some of the stalls sold scrap metal, much of it abandoned shells and chunks of weaponry. War had been over for forty years, but forgotten landmines were still taking the legs and lives of Vietnamese farmers.

Many of the women wore white full-length *ao dai* dresses, simple and elegant with a high collar, fitted bodice and loose skirt. She couldn't believe anyone could keep an outfit like that clean in this city. The men wore dark blue pyjama-like outfits or T-shirts and shorts. Sinter dressed as she had in her native India: a dark-coloured T-shirt which wouldn't show splashes of mud or blood, inevitable with her new job, and jeans that could be boil-washed every other day and not fall apart.

Sinter had been in Vietnam for three months, and had taken Ho Chi Minh to her heart. It was a dirty, polluted city, phenomenally noisy with the high-pitched roar of mopeds. These were used as transport for the entire household, with a whole family of five squeezed onto one moped! Despite its downfalls, the city had history, beauty, and people who needed help. It was also a place where a runaway could vanish without trace. Sinter had arrived on a forged passport, alone and eager to disappear into the mêlée of millions. To begin with it had been so exciting. She had felt like an international woman of mystery, on the run from a dread organisation that wanted her silenced. She'd changed hostels every few nights, leaving different names, covering her tracks at every turn. One night, she'd been walking through a market, and saw a slender young man with close-cropped hair. Her stomach leapt with horror; the Clan had found her! Instantly she'd found herself running through a mental checklist like Saker would have done; "he hasn't noticed that you've spotted him – use surprise and the public situation to your advantage . . . the best form of defence can be attack."

Sinter had dropped her shoulder and charged the food cart in front of her, driving it right into the young man, knocking him flat on his back. The stallholders yelled out in fury. In the chaos Sinter turned and ran. Seconds later she risked a glance over her shoulder, and saw the young man helping up the food-cart owner with a look of genuine bewilderment on his face. In a second, she could see she'd made a mistake. He wasn't Clan; he was just a traveller wandering the night market in search of trinkets. That night she lay on her hostel bed, furious with herself for being so paranoid.

After a few months of imagining skulking assassins in every shadow, it became clear no one had come looking for her. She really was forgotten, alone in a city of millions of souls. Sinter had parted company from her friend Saker months before, and he had since been totally silent, with no contact whatsoever. It was as if their whole adventure had been a bizarre dream – or a nightmare. Occasionally she wondered what had happened to him, was he thinking of her too? Wherever he was, she was sure that he was embroiled in some kind of insane intrigue, and felt a twinge every time she faced the possibility that the Clan might have caught up with him.

She was trying to be frugal, eating in the markets with the local tradesmen and staying in the most rundown hostels, but the dollars Saker had shared with her ran dry.

She was going to have to find a job. This was harder than it sounded. What kind of job could an eighteen-year-old Indian girl with no spoken Vietnamese, and no qualifications, do? And eighteen years old was only what it said on her forged passport, actually she was still not even fifteen.

Her first thought had been to teach English. Hindi had been the main language around the tea plantation back home, but like all Indian girls of her upbringing Sinter spoke and wrote English more correctly than any British or American girl. All she needed was something to prove it. It was alarmingly simple to buy a fancy-looking piece of paper from a street forger, proving she had an English degree from Mumbai University. Sinter had to laugh; to have a degree she'd have had to be over twenty years old! It turned out that was not going to be a problem. In Ho Chi Minh English was taught by teachers who had never even met an English person, and was spoken quite incredibly badly. Schools were so desperate for teachers that Sinter could have turned up with a degree certificate written on the back of a greasy napkin and they'd have hired her on the spot.

Sinter's first class had been terrifying. There'd been no classroom, instead, it took place in a bar, deserted in the daytime, smelling like an unwashed toilet. All along the walls were shelves lined with bottles of whisky filled with grotesque twists of ginseng and pickled cobras, apparently supposed to endow the drinker with great strength. There were maybe fifteen students, all of them older than her, and none spoke a word of English. At first she thought they'd treat a girl of her age with disdain, but Asian cultures respect teachers greatly. She read to them from an English book, and had them repeat words for objects from apples to microwave ovens. At the end of every day, she'd head back to a cheap dorm room. The place had a constantly changing barrage of travellers and vagrants. Occasionally she'd share a conversation, but they soon sensed Sinter didn't want to talk about herself. She felt she had to guard her story closely. If she was found out she risked being apprehended and taken home in disgrace or, worse, having the Clan swoop in the night. It was far better to be anonymous and lonely. No one stayed at the hostel longer than a night or two, so she made no friends. Sometimes she'd lie in bed at night, staring at the mouldy ceiling and having to fight back tears.

However, as an Indian of high-class Brahmin upbringing, Sinter's pride wouldn't let her feel sorry for herself for long. She soon tired of reciting parrot-fashion phrases to her students. She had escaped from India to find her purpose in life, and this wasn't it. One day when she had no work planned, she decided to explore some parts of the city she hadn't yet visited, and wandered into the really poor area of town. The buildings here were on stilts over the water, so litter and toilets could just empty straight into the black greasy fluid below. The houses were mostly constructed of metal sheets, and in the midday sun heated up like sweatboxes.

It doesn't matter where in the world, whether it's the townships of South Africa, the *favelas* of Brazil or the slums of Calcutta, the places where the most impoverished people live are a mix of activity and life, with loud music and shouted arguments taking place on doorsteps. Children chatter and play around open drains flowing with effluence and rubbish. Human beings are packed together shoulder to shoulder, living every aspect of their lives in roughly assembled shanty towns that look as if a stiff breeze might blow them over. Often there is a tight sense of community, with the inhabitants taking care of their own, and it is generally a bad idea for an outsider to be there unguided.

Sinter sensed staring eyes following her every move. Carefully she picked her way along boardwalks, certainly not wanting to miss her step and tumble into any of the open sewers. In the heart of the town, Sinter had to press herself to the wall on one side of the gangway in order to avoid a queue of people who were waiting patiently on the boardwalk. At the end of the queue was a small shack with a roof made of corrugated iron, and walls of blankets hung over washing lines. Inside were two picnic tables, one of which held a steaming cauldron of some tantalising food, which was being served up by a stern-looking Vietnamese woman wearing a stained apron. At the other table, sitting behind several plastic boxes of medical supplies, sat a harried-looking red-haired lady covered in freckles. Sinter estimated that she was in her late twenties. She was jabbing a hypodermic needle into a baby while her mother looked on, terrified. As Sinter peered in under the corrugated ceiling the redhead looked up, barking out a question in Vietnamese. Sinter shook her head, to show that she didn't understand. The redhead looked exasperated, and tried again in English.

"The queue starts way back there, you know? What do you want?"

Sinter responded with a silent shrug. She didn't quite know what she wanted!

"Just another tourist come for a gawp, are ya?" cursed the lady. "I reckon they'll start bringing sightseeing coaches through here soon."

Sinter shook her head vigorously. "No ma'am, I'm very sorry. I was just wondering what this place is."

"What does it look like? These people need sorting out, so we help them, simple as that." Sinter was having trouble placing the accent. Australian? No, not quite. Irish, perhaps?

"And you are a doctor?" Sinter asked, trying not to sound too awestruck. The Irish woman sighed, wiping the screaming baby's injection wound with an alcohol wipe.

"Doctor of lost causes perhaps . . . Nah. I tried for Médicins Sans Frontières . . ." she registered Sinter's blank look and translated, "that's Doctors without Borders."

Sinter was still looking blank, so she continued, "but they wouldn't take me; they just wanted fully qualified surgeons. I tried just about everyone, no luck. So, it's just me." And then gesturing around her at the rickety shelter, "Me and my palace of delights."

She then looked at Sinter inquisitively. "Aren't you a little bit young to be walking round here on your own?"

"I'm eighteen years old," Sinter retorted a little too quickly and defensively. Then, nodding at the syringe in the redhead's fingers, "and I know how to give injections."

The redhead looked at Sinter with an expression somewhere between quizzical and interested.

It turned out that the good Samaritan was called Roisin, pronounced "Rosheen", and was indeed Irish. She was also desperately in need of helping hands. Sinter donned an apron straight away, and was dressing minor wounds and serving soup within the hour. By the end of the day Roisin had shown her how to put in a saline drip, and talked her through the basic drugs they had. Roisin never asked Sinter anything about where she had come from, who she was, and what her plans were. Before Sinter knew it, the day was done, and she hadn't thought once about the Clan, about her father, about Saker, about the future. All she'd thought about was the queue of people who needed her help.

Sinter and Roisin shook hands and parted without making any plan to meet again. Yet the very next morning Sinter skipped her teaching job and went back to the little shack, to spend her day administering antibiotics, teaching mums how to use mosquito nets to keep their babies safe from malaria, and how to clean wounds so they wouldn't become infected. It was a mix of horror and heartache, spiced with the most extraordinary highs. But perhaps best of all, the day had a purpose, and passed in the blink of an eye. As she returned to the hostel, she suddenly realised she was singing an old Bollywood tune she hadn't thought about since she'd left home.

From then on, she was at the shelter every day. Sometimes a mother whose baby's fever had been quelled would return with a cloth filled with warm dumplings as a gift. Or a stiff old man would shake her hands with tears in his eyes, delighted to have been given some respite from a bad back or crooked knees.

Eventually, after a month helping out, they had finished a hard day, and were sitting on the steps of Roisin's small apartment on the edge of the shanties sharing a baguette and some pâté. Vietnam had been a French colony for many years, and even in the poorest areas of town good warm bread was available on any street corner. Sinter tore open the fresh baguette, drinking in the doughy smell and salivating.

Roisin turned her green eyes to Sinter as if sizing her up, and spoke.

"So, Missy, I've just had an email from one of the donors back home in Ireland. He kind of sits around waiting for old widows to die, and gets 'em to leave us everything in their wills." Working in the shanty had given Roisin something of a black sense of humour.

"Anyway, one has just passed on, and left us a bit of a jackpot. Enough to keep this place going for a year or two, any road."

Sinter turned to Roisin, wide-eyed. "That's great – you can get a proper building! Or maybe get some more equipment! It's going to be fantastic."

Roisin turned away, a serious look on her face, and Sinter's heart plummeted. Perhaps Roisin was thinking of moving back to Ireland? Or maybe now that she had funding she would be looking to get a proper doctor, and Sinter would be surplus to requirements.

"Well, yeah. I could do that. Or I suppose I could get meself some Jimmy Choos and head for the Riviera, Monaco maybe . . ."

Roisin looked down at her muddy jeans and mountain boots, smeared with unspeakable grime, and added sardonically, "I'd fit in perfect."

"But I reckon what I really need is an apprentice." Roisin sat back, and took a swig from a plastic cup of warm beer, allowing the thought to sink in. "I couldn't pay much, but if you moved in here with me you wouldn't need that much money. You're so skinny I doubt you'll be eating me out of bread!" Sinter was silent so she continued, "There's a little spare room. Next door's cockerels start their screaming about four in the morning, so you'd best get some earplugs. And actually, I say room, but it's not much more than a cupboard . . . guess you can always sleep sitting up!" She smiled to show that this was a joke.

Then was totally serious. "No, honestly, it's a rubbish room."

Sinter's silence was by now starting to become off-putting but Roisin continued, "It's only an offer; think about it for as long as you like."

But Sinter didn't need to think about it. "You're asking me? To come and work for you? But, it's . . . I . . ." and, without knowing why, she burst into tears.

"Hey! It's OK! You don't have to stay with me," Roisin went from amused to bewildered. "I mean, I know I smell bad now, but that's just the sweat. Are you OK?"

"Of course, yes. It's all I've ever wanted. It's perfect. Thank you." And then through her tears, "When can I start?"

"Steady on there, Tonto," replied Roisin. "There'll be plenty of time for mopping up blood and baby puke. Are ya finishing that pâté now? That's top-quality rat meat that, you know!" The two looked around and laughed out loud.

3

Underneath the Bornean forest canopy, Saker tried to pack Leysin's wound with spongy sphagnum moss, tying torn strands of palm leaf around the dressing to hold it in place.

The bullet had gone in below the shoulder blade, leaving a small wound, but it had flattened as it exited, leaving a gory hole torn through his rib cage. Mercifully it had missed Leysin's heart, but had certainly gone through his lung. His blood was frothing with every breath. He needed to get to a hospital and soon.

"I wish Sinter was here; she'd know how to deal with this," Saker found himself muttering, as he tried to staunch the flow of blood from the man's chest. There was a tiny twinge in his conscience as he thought of Sinter, and a lurch in his heart as well. It had been months now, and he hadn't made any attempt to watch over her as he had promised he would. He didn't even know which country she was in; had she returned to India? Or gone somewhere else entirely? He shook his head, annoyed at himself. There were more pressing responsibilities to take care of.

They had battled two kilometres away from the loggers' clearing before his Penan friend had collapsed, unable to go any further. Though the hunter was only slight in build, and shorter than Saker, Saker would not be able to carry him. Certainly not through this terrain. The jungles of Sarawak in northern Borneo lie on limestone foundations, spiky white rock stained green with algae. Saker had learned quickly that where the rock sticks up through the dead leaves of the forest floor it is utterly treacherous, slippery to walk on, and with lethal points standing like spears to impale you should you fall.

Saker crouched alongside the Penan, and put his palm on his forehead.

"It's OK, everything's going to be cool. We'll be munching mangoes by breakfast," he reassured him, not believing his own words. The rest of the Penan had spent the previous night perhaps five kilometres away. It would be an easy hour's walk on decent ground. Over this forest terrain it might be two hours, but for Saker bearing a wounded man on his own . . . well, it could take days.

Saker took up his knife, and trotted off into the trees. Leysin sat up in panic, calling out not to be left alone, but soon Saker returned, with two stout staves cut from perfectly straight saplings. Here on the forest floor it was always dark, with the canopy above cutting out access to the sun. Trees need sunlight, so for the first few years of their lives rainforest trees grow bolt upright, with no branches, racing to find sunlight. The trunks are like telegraph poles and make for wonderful building materials. Placing the two staves side by side, Saker wove a wickerwork sheet from palm fronds, and tied it between the two, creating a makeshift stretcher. He heaved Leysin on, picked up the handles at one end as if dragging a wheelbarrow, and started to tow his wounded companion along the game path that led towards the Penan's camp.

Saker pulled through the night. Where the limestone poked up through the dirt, it was an assault course. He'd be able to pull for a hundred metres before he thought he would simply have to lie down and die. At other times he'd encounter good soft trails on flat ground, and might do eight hundred metres in an hour. Every now and again he'd slake his thirst at a stream, moisten Leysin's lips and dampen his forehead. Finally, as his energy seemed spent, there was a vague change to the forest. Suddenly the fruit doves and oropendolas were beginning their fluted calls, and eventually they were joined by the mournful whooping song of a distant gibbon. Dawn was close. In the half-light, direction finding became easier, and when sun finally pierced the gloom, Saker stood in a shaft of golden light as if he was under a hot shower after a walk in a winter downpour. He felt the life returning to his fingertips, the energy start to zing in his veins, and he took up the stretcher with renewed vigour.

It was around eight in the morning when he got to the Penan camp. There were six box-like structures on bamboo stilts, thatched roofs but no walls. The Penan were so skilled that they could construct a camp like this in less than a day. On the floor, naked, dirty-faced babies crawled around their mothers as they prepared sago paste or crushed up pulses and seeds for the next meal. The warriors sat sullen, smoking fragrant tobacco rolled in slices of banana leaf. They glowered at Saker as they took the stretcher from him, and carried Leysin off to be treated. They didn't speak, but it was clear from their body language that Saker had done something terrible indeed. For his part, Saker could have cried with relief to find them still there.

Whatever happened, Saker had to make his peace with the Penan. When he and Sinter had gone their separate ways, he'd been without purpose, totally cast adrift. And then he'd heard of the Penan, the Ghosts of the Forest, living their shadowy life in northern Borneo. It was as if a light had gone on in his head, and he'd known he had to join them. In the few months since he'd been with them, he'd found exactly the sense of family and mutual purpose that he'd had with the Clan. Like the Clan, his new brothers lived in harmony with the forest. Every day he was sucking up knowledge about how the jungle could feed, clothe and provide everything necessary for life. The difference was that the Penan's code was peaceful; they hated conflict. Fleeing his childhood in the Clan, it was everything Saker needed.

The Penan are one of very few peoples in the world who still live hunter-gatherer lifestyles, as they have for millennia. They are nomads, always on the move, living in a hunting camp for a few weeks before moving on. This prevents them from over-exploiting any patch of forest. They return to each new jungle grove as if revisiting an old friend, seeking out hunting grounds that have been passed down for generations. The animals they share the forests with are like brothers, and some possess the spirits of their ancestors. Most treasured of all is the silent ape in the treetops, the orang utan. The Penan see the old man of the forest as one of their own. No matter how desperate the hunger might be, no one would ever draw their bow against an orang utan; that would be like assaulting a member of their own family. The first time Saker saw one, it was a female nursing an infant at her breast, eyes cast upwards as if she was smiling. He saw in her dark eyes his own past, present and future. She looked so wise, without cares, so tranquil. And like a human mother, her arms were wrapped around her baby, using her body to protect it from harm. He was completely riveted.

Suddenly in those precious seconds it all became clear. It was so simple. He had been searching for a purpose – well, here it was! To do whatever he could to protect these forests for his new friends, and for the orang utans. Just as the mother ape would give her life to save her baby, he had to be prepared to lay down his life for his new family.

The sad fact was that one life would most certainly not be enough. In recent years, the Penan were coming home to treasured forests and finding them hacked down. Timber, land and crops were big business, and the lives of a few thousand quiet forest dwellers and orang utans were just an annoyance to those with money to make. As the forests shrank beneath the loggers' trucks and chainsaws, they had nowhere left to move to. The orang utans were even more tied to the forest than the Penan. They couldn't live in plantations or in the squalid settlements the government tried to force the Penan to move into. These gentle primates were being squeezed out of existence, as surely as their brothers the Penan.

It had taken many weeks of quiet determination for Saker to be accepted by the Penan. First of all he had tracked them through the forest. This had been near impossible, as the Penan were far more skilful at concealing their presence than Saker was at following them. However, as the Penan moved, they left signs on the trail for other members of their tribe: the midrib of a folded leaf pointing in their direction of travel; a single stick notched in four places signalled a party of four people; a seemingly random berry showed that the party was looking for wild fruits. Saker didn't fully understand the language, but he'd followed the signs avidly, knowing he was being watched and measured by invisible eyes. Eventually the tribe determined he was alone and harmless, and one morning he'd woken to find he'd been given a gift. A leather thong had been tied round his ankle as he slept. The invisible visitors had also scratched a symbol in the ashes of his fire, which seemed to be giving him directions. Cautiously Saker had followed them to a crystal-clear stream. As he knelt to drink, the riverbanks suddenly came alive with the faces that had haunted his every step. The Penan were wary, but had allowed him to tag along. Day by day he had won their confidence, convincing the elders that he shared their passion, and indeed wanted to offer them help.

For the following months, he kept quiet, and tried to live like his hosts. He ate what they ate, slept when they slept, studied every move and movement. He stunned palm-sized fish in the creeks using poisons made from mashed-up tree bark, and toasted them over the open flames using spindly sticks as spits. They seemed to be all needle-sharp bones that stuck in the roof of his mouth, and pitiful amounts of flesh, but he knew every tiny chunk of protein was valuable. In the evening he became a human climbing frame for the babies of the village, who clambered over him with their soot-blackened fingers in his ears and up his nose. Sometimes they were so like their orang utan brothers it was plain scary! Saker was treated with patience and kindness, but almost like a small child. When he added the wrong leaves to a stew and ruined it, they didn't scold him, but didn't give him the job again for several weeks. He would rather have been told off.

To most boys of fifteen, born in the Western world, this lifestyle would have been impossibly slow, and fraught with hardship. But because Saker's early life had been far from conventional, to him it seemed perfectly normal. It was still unclear when and where he had been born, and he had no knowledge of his parents. He had no memories whatsoever of anything before the age of five or six years old. His life after that was so bizarre that it barely seemed real. Saker had been brought up by a different kind of tribe, a band of young men called the Clan, taught by a sinister collective of teachers led by a man known only as the Prophet. The Clan were immersed in a range of skills, from picking pockets to bush lore, and from martial arts to disguise. Each was linked to their own totem animal – the cottonmouth, the mongoose, the wolf. The Clan boys took on the name of their totem, would have their image tattooed on their body, would learn their skills, and study their deadly techniques. While the Penan were brothers with a gentle ape that lived quiet and harmless in the treetops, the Clan chose totem animals for their predatory prowess: the wolf, the pit viper, the harpy eagle and the panther. His namesake was the lethal Saker falcon, dark-eyed, swift, precise. He had been well named.

When members of the Clan were old enough, their considerable skills were auctioned off to the highest bidder. As far as Saker could see, they were never hired out for anything moral. They were destined to be thieves, spies, even assassins. Some of the boys never returned from their missions. After Saker had been part of a unit that was sent out to kill endangered tigers, he finally shook off his brainwashing and ran. It had been a crime that seemed to contradict everything he felt and believed, and he had been running ever since.

Fortune had crossed his path with Sinter, a young Indian girl of high breeding, who had unexpectedly turned out to be a willing runaway. For a while it had seemed the two of them might make a good team, but . . . Saker shook his head to clear the image. Sinter was far away now, and must be glad to be rid of him. Now he had the Penan, and they were all the friends he needed. Friends? No, they were family, his future . . . but in the loggers' camp he'd broken their rules and destroyed their trust.

While Saker piled a plateful of smoky deer meat and sago porridge into his mouth, the Penan held council. Their near-naked figures made a striking sight sitting in a circle around the smouldering fire, particularly as they were still wearing their body paints from the previous night. Each took their turn to speak, with the chief chairing the discussion. The first difficult question was whether they should take Leysin out of the forest to a hospital. There was no doubt that his wounds were beyond the treatment of their jungle remedies. The second question was what to do with Saker.

The group argued for about an hour. Every few minutes

one would leap to his feet and start shouting and gesticulating, clearly stating that Saker should be outcast or worse. As the shouting heightened, another word was repeated more and more often, a foreign name that didn't fit in their language. "Lars", they kept saying, as if referring to some exotic god. Eventually they seemed to reach a decision, and two men left the group. They didn't take their blowpipes, but carried a small wrap of cloth filled with deer meat. Saker guessed this meant they were intending to be gone for a while, but were not hunting.

He'd heard the legend of Lars Hagen when he was seeking the Penan. Hagen was a Swiss journalist who had come to Borneo to meet the Penan, and had ended up living with them, passionately taking up their cause. It was he who encouraged them to set up blockades in front of the logging vehicles, and took their protests to the outside world. Hagen attracted the attention of the press, but also of the Malaysian government and logging companies. Not surprisingly, they tried to have him thrown out of the country. He had done more than anyone to mobilise these peaceful people. He showed them how to protect their heritage, and made a complete nuisance of himself with the powerful companies destroying the forest. Then suddenly, abruptly, he'd vanished. The Malaysian government said he was lost in the mountains, but no one believed that. Hagen had lived for a decade with the Penan, and knew the ways of their forests intimately. Many believed the troublesome freedom-fighter had been silenced by a logger's rifle. Others thought he'd just disappeared into his beloved jungle, and continued to live far from the evils of the modern world. Saker didn't know the truth, but wondered if perhaps the Penan had gone to find Lars, and seek his advice.

By the end of that day, Saker had eaten his fill many times over, snoozed under a palm shelter and regained the strength spent in his night of effort. The Penan women – their cut earlobes hanging to their shoulders like great hooped earrings – tended to his needs, but wouldn't address any of his questions, and would merely tut at him as they would to one of their naughty pigs.

Saker had long ago shed all the trappings of the modern world, including a wristwatch. He had learned to tell the time from the sights and sounds of the world around him. The day began with the whoop of the gibbons, soon overtaken by the chuckling, babbling brook song of the straw-headed bulbul. The middle of the day was marked by the long tone of the magpie robin, often lazy and monotone, then occasionally surprised and rising in inflection; fluted notes that sounded as if the bird was trying to sing with a dewdrop of water in its throat. As dusk approached, the melodious white-rumped shama would set to singing, trying to overpower the bush crickets. If it had rained, the frogs would also be battling to be heard, with chirps, squeaks, croaks and "bonk" sounds. Then the largest and noisiest cicada began its clamour. The sound was deafening, as loud as an industrial bandsaw, and sounded like a fire engine. It began every evening at bang on six o'clock, so precise that he could have set his watch by it . . . if he had one. Occasionally the insects themselves would come into the firelight. They were enormous, as big as a clenched human fist, with red eyes the size of garden peas, and huge stained-glass window wings clasped over their backs. The males buzzed in his hand like some kind of vibrating toy, as they fought to sing to attract a mate. For the first few weeks their incessant song drove him insane, and he thought he would never sleep. Now he found it comforting.

Long after the cicadas had started blaring, Saker was dozing fitfully, his dreaming mind filled with images of Penan hunters dancing around a flickering fire, sprites of light dancing heavenwards. Their warpaint started to morph into animal tattoos, their faces to form the shapes of the young men of the Clan: Raven, a glossy, black-haired boy of keen intelligence, sprang along the ground, his two feet side by side. When he opened his mouth, all that came out was the cronking call of the mightiest of crows. Taipan was a lithe youngster, gyrating in the firelight. As Saker's mind's eye zoomed in on him, the tattoo that covered the entirety of his chest came to life, a great snake erupting from his flesh, and becoming a hissing hell in scales. And there, in the middle of the fire, was a writhing figure, his face replaced by his Clan tattoo, which was a monochrome bird of prey screaming out with an ugly caw. At his feet in the flames lay the orange and black striped shape of a tiger, its amber eyes imploring mercy, but the falcon boy paid no heed, he raised a great dagger in his hands and drove it home. The dancing figures of the Clan exploded in an orgy of excitement, chanting a cacophony of vile animal calls, like a nightmare zoo gone mad. And then far-off voices started to echo, merging with the calls of the Clan, and suddenly all of the dancing figures were chanting; "Lars, Lars, Lars!"

Saker kicked out his leg in a sleep-twitch, waking himself up. He sat upright, the images of the Clan gone, the chants still there.

"Lars, Lars, Lars!" the Penan were yelling. Reality had gatecrashed his dream.

In front of the campfire, men and women were clustered around a tall, dark-haired figure. His skin was nut-brown and wrinkled from many years in the tropics, but there was no doubt he was not of Penan origin. It was really him: the man of legend.

Lars Hagen nodded to Saker, the only Westerner he had encountered in over a decade. Then he sat next to the fire, took a bamboo cup of palm wine, and began to talk with the elders. They talked long into the night, while Saker sat under his palm shelter feeling like a naughty schoolboy, utterly left out. It did however give him the chance to assess from a distance the man he had heard so much about. Hagen wore round spectacles, hair short on top, but long around the temples, and with the suggestion of a beard. He had an air of unmistakable authority. Even the medicine man and tribal Big Man bowed their assent whenever he spoke. They smoked and sipped a milky liquor, distilled from palm sap. Hagen talked in the Penan language with no accent. Finally the group came to a conclusion and stood. Six Penan bore Leysin off on his stretcher, taking him out of the forest and to hospital. Hagen walked across to Saker and stood in front of him, sizing him up, not offering his hand to shake.

"So this is a real mess you've managed to create here," he said finally. "I think perhaps you and I should take a little walk."

They walked silently through the moonlit forest. Saker had so many questions he wanted to ask, but Hagen's demeanour didn't encourage any small talk. Eventually they reached a steep cliff face and slogged upwards, slipping through the mud, using vines and roots as handholds. After an hour or so of climbing the gradient slackened, and they found themselves in a dense forest of spindly trees. Saker couldn't believe how hard it was to keep pace with the older man, who seemed to glide through the undergrowth while Saker battled against it as if the bushes were made of barbed wire. Abruptly they broke out of the thick vegetation, and in the half-light Saker had to stifle a yell. He had nearly stepped into a giant, seemingly bottomless, hole. They were teetering on the edge of a mighty sinkhole, perfectly circular, as broad across as two football fields. The depth was impossible to estimate, but a mighty white stalactite hanging from the rim of the cave was as long as a five-storey building. It was the most awe-inspiring thing Saker had ever seen. Hagen turned to him and spoke.

"I'm not sure what it is you're searching for, Saker. I can tell there is something black in your past, and you feel that by helping these people you can make yourself whole. But you can't help them, or the forest brothers, with a heart full of anger. You need to understand how this world works." He made a sweeping gesture that took in everything around them.

"I do understand!" protested Saker. "I hate the loggers as much as anyone."

"No!" interrupted Hagen. "This is not about hate. Hate breeds more hate, your anger won't save the Penan or their forests."

"Well, what will?" shouted Saker, by now starting to feel pretty unappreciated, and not a little patronised. "What good has it done you just disappearing into the forest? You were making a difference, people were listening to you, and then you just went and deserted them! If you're so smart, why won't you show me what I have to do?"

Hagen breathed out with world-weary bitter patience. "My efforts had become too . . . political. I was doing the Penan and the orang utans more harm than good. Mercenaries followed me to shut me up, and ended up killing any Penan they found instead. They killed anyone who'd helped me, anyone who knew me, anyone who had even heard of me. Orangs were slaughtered in the treetops and their infants carted off to zoos, or to be pets for spoilt rich girls. Too many people I loved were getting hurt; it was better for me to . . . disappear. The press could make me a martyr, and the bad men could take a break from killing the Penan."

"You may have given up," said Saker, "but I'm not ready to do that yet. Why can't you teach me what I have to do?"

Hagen took a deep breath. "Saker, you can learn about the plants, about the animals, even about how to take a life. But this lesson can't be taught." He broke a twig from a nearby tree and tossed it into the sinkhole. It spiralled away into the depths like a falling helicopter. There was no sound of it hitting the bottom. "Your answers are down there."

4

Halfway through giving a mother her tetanus shot, Sinter saw him. Perhaps because he was wearing a sweatshirt with the hood pulled up, despite the fact that it was midday in Ho Chi Minh and as hot as a sauna. Perhaps it was the thick dark eyebrows, or the fact that he was too tall and too muscular to blend into a Vietnamese crowd. A yelp of pain from her patient brought Sinter back to reality, and she apologised, wiping the botched injection wound clean. When she looked back to the entrance of the shelter, the young man was gone. She shook her head. Perhaps it was just the heat inside the little shack. Or maybe she was just a bit overworked and seeing things. But it wasn't the first time she'd seen lurking shadows in the last few days.

Since the large donation, the shelter had gone from strength to strength. Roisin had been able to wangle a big consignment of drugs from a French hospital. They were past their expiry date, and should have been thrown away, but would still work, so one of the doctors had sneaked them out, and sent them to Roisin. Sinter had managed to get a computer set up in the flat, so that they could search the internet for even more potential donors. After a few weeks of sleepless nights, she'd also persuaded the next-door neighbours to make their cockerel into a tasty stew. She'd made the tiny box room in Roisin's house feel quite homely, with a little herb garden in the windowbox, and posters of Bollywood stars on her walls to remind her of home. She and Roisin were inseparable, and had become like family, but they still hadn't discussed anything about Sinter's past. Sinter was getting used to living entirely in a constructed world, and was seriously thinking about forging qualifications, so she could realise her dream of going to medical school and becoming a doctor for real. It was all too wonderful, and she had never, ever been happier. That was until she started to see the faces.

Some of their work involved leaving the centre, and going out into the city to the people that needed their help most. It was always quite a relief to leave the crowded, sweaty shack, so they took it in turns to head down to the riverside, where they'd chat to the women washing their laundry in the grotty waters of the Mekong. They'd encourage the women to bring their children to get injections, or to come and have small wounds dressed before they got infected. One day Sinter was laughing with a group of brightly dressed old women, when something out of the ordinary caught her eye. On the other side of the river, a foreigner was taking photos of them with a long zoom lens. She wasn't sure what caught her attention. Tourists were not unknown in that part of the city, and they often had far more conspicuous clothing than this young man. It wasn't that – it was something about his bearing, a shoulders-thrown-back confidence that only athletes and fighters possess. And the fact that as soon as he realised she had spotted him, he turned on his heel and strode up the bank.

"Hey, you!" she shouted, but he didn't stop, just vanished into the crowds on the other side of the river.

Next time it happened, Sinter was in a three-wheel *tuktuk* scooter taxi, dodging in between trucks and the cows that wander the Vietnamese streets. Saker had taught her to always check the mirrors when in a vehicle. If you registered the same car in your rear-view mirror after three separate manoeuvres, it was following you. Over the last few months Sinter's paranoia had faded, and she no longer bothered with such silliness. However, today, there was something about another blue *tuktuk* just behind her that caught her attention. It slowed when they slowed, and sped up too fast in order to get through a traffic signal and keep on their tail. They turned towards the central square and she looked back. Still there. Then they took a left when a policeman in the centre of the road was clearly telling them to go right. She glanced in the mirror. It was still there.

"Take the next right," she instructed the driver, and he wrenched the wheel to the right, zipping down a street congested with pedestrians. They ground to a halt, and the blue *tuktuk* pulled up alongside them. Sinter caught a glimpse of the passenger, and the breath caught in her throat.

"Saker!" she yelled, then faltered. The passenger had the same cropped hair, the same physique and hooked nose, but it wasn't him. Sinter made to leap out of the *tuktuk*, but the throng of people was too dense. She barged her way past a man bearing sweetmeats on a pole across his shoulders, and almost pushed a hobbling old man to the ground to get to the blue *tuktuk*. She grabbed hold of the old man just in time and, apologising, pulled him back to his feet. When she turned back to the blue vehicle, the passenger seat was empty.

"Where did he go?" she yelled at the driver, but he shook his head, showing he didn't understand.

"What did he pay you? Where did you pick him up?" But by now she was overcome by the crowd, and her own *tuktuk* driver complaining that she'd run off without paying. Mystery man had vanished.

That night, Sinter lay in her tiny bed, in her tiny bedroom. The barking of fighting dogs, "tokay" calls from the bright blue and orange geckos hunting moths around her light, and the creak of her ancient fan were the soundtrack to her evening. Alongside her bed, on the upturned fruit crate she used as a bedside table, sat a mobile phone. It was the one link between her and the only person in the world who knew her true past. She lifted her trouser leg, and revealed the black tattoo snarling on her calf. "The Tigress", Saker had called her, and she had glowed with pride. He had told Sinter that he would always be able to find her, and she had believed him. Back then he had seemed infallible. Now that they had been apart for so long, he was just one boy, in a very big world. He would never be able to find her. This phone was their only connection.

They had stayed together nearly a month after escaping from the walled citadel in the Himalayas, making their way down into the lowlands, arriving at a small city where they'd taken a couple of rooms in a dingy hotel. The closer they'd got to civilisation, the more cranky Saker had become. His moods would swing from cheery, to looking like a thundercloud that was about to burst. Sometimes he wouldn't talk to Sinter for a whole day. To begin with, she'd put up with his moods. He was the only friend she had left in the world, but was clearly haunted by demons he didn't want to talk about. He was battling to piece together all the parts of the puzzle, of the Clan and his dark history. He had no time for conversation.

When thrown together by their adventure, they had formed an uneasy bond, an alliance. But now that there was no reason for them to be a partnership any more, the alliance was faltering. Despite all she'd learned from Saker, despite the fact that she owed her life to him, she found the boy unbearable. He was so caught up in his obsession with his past that he couldn't see the present. That meant simply not thinking about anyone else, and certainly not Sinter. But she had problems too. After all, she had found out that her own father had wanted to sell her to a villain – the same villain who was destroying tigers for money. She could never go home to India and her privileged upbringing, and was as lost as he was.

Sinter was too strong and too proud to confront Saker about it, and made up her mind to tell him she was leaving.

"I think it's time we went our separate ways," she said. "I've booked myself on a bus to Bangladesh. I leave for Dhaka tomorrow morning."

Saker looked up with surprise, his hooded eyes surveying her as if trying to figure out what she was thinking. Eventually he responded, "That's a good idea. We should split up for a while. It will be harder for them to track us if we're working in different areas."

"What are you talking about?" she asked. "We're not working. To me it just looks like we're hiding, wasting our time, we can't go on like this for ever."

"Of course not," he responded. "But we still need to keep a low profile, we don't want to draw attention to ourselves. They'll be watching."

"They? Who are they? And why do you think you're so important that *they* are going to follow you wherever the hell you go? Your Clan will have gone back to torturing animals for the highest bidder, they'll have forgotten all about you."

Saker snorted. He knew that wasn't true. The Clan would never forget him, not while he still had breath in his body, and so much ammunition against them. Why couldn't she understand that?

"Face it, you're not a shady assassin any more, you're just a boy." She had to bite her lip not to add, "With an attitude problem."

"So what's your big plan then?" Saker retorted. "You going to save the world all by yourself?"

"We can't lie low for ever. I want to get on with my life." Sinter was doing her best not to sound petulant. "And I'm not talking about splitting 'for a while' as some kind of tactical manoeuvre. I'm going. For good. I don't know where yet, but it'll be better than this."

Her gesture took in everything around them, the shoddy hotel, the cockroaches under the table at breakfast, and Saker himself. Saker was stunned, but he wasn't going to let Sinter see that he was hurt. He didn't even try to talk her out of it. In fact, he told himself he would be glad to see the back of her. However, as she was fighting her way onto the bus, she felt him touch her upper arm. Something was pressed into her hand.

"Take this," he said. "It's a phone, quadband; you can use it anywhere in the world. If you need me, if anything happens, if they . . ." his voice trailed off. He couldn't meet her amber-eyed gaze.

"There's a number in the contacts, under 'taxi cabs'. Just call it, and leave me a message saying exactly where you are. Lats and longs if possible." She knew that meant latitude and longitude, the global grid reference that makes it possible to mark any spot on the planet. "You don't need to say anything else," he continued. "I'll be there as soon as I can."

"And what if you want to find me?" Sinter asked, taken off guard.

"If I want to, I'll find you," he replied, in a way that seemed to suggest that was unlikely.

"Saker . . ." she began, then stopped herself. She wanted to tell him to stop being such a spoilt child, to stop thinking he was the only person in the world with problems. She wanted to tell him that his obsession with the Clan was going to destroy him, that sooner or later he would have to find something else in his life. And that perhaps he ought to value the one friend and ally he had left. Instead, she silently took the phone, flicked her black hair out of her eyes, and without a backward glance stepped into the bus.

That had been many moons ago now. She had made her way overland all the way to Vietnam, growing in confidence every day. She had covered thousands of miles through the sweltering lowlands of Bangladesh, the mountains of Burma, and through the temples and cities of Thailand, and now here she was, living out her dream of becoming a doctor, and barely ever thinking of the past. She groaned inwardly to herself. Sure, he had been insufferable and self-centred, but life had certainly been more exciting since he'd come along. She picked up the phone, scrolled down to the number that read "taxi cabs" and pondered, before tossing it back onto her bedside table.

Dawn, and Sinter woke in a cold sweat, gripped with fear. Rolling over onto her side, the phone on her bedside table seemed to be mocking her. She picked it up, and tossed it into the bin in the corner of her tiny room, where it dropped in among the waste paper with a satisfying plop.

"Three points!" she cheered, with a pleasure she didn't feel.

Still wearing the pyjamas Roisin had given her, she walked to the kitchen to get a glass of water and leapt with shock. A young boy was sitting at their new computer, tapping away furiously on the keys, focused with extraordinary intensity on the screen in front of him. His dark floppy hair kept slipping into his eyes as he typed, and he'd repeatedly shake his head in a kind of twitch to clear his vision.

"Who are you?" Sinter demanded. The boy didn't even register her presence. "Answer me, what are you doing here?"

He totally ignored her, his brow furrowed in concentration. This was just plain bizarre. Sinter pondered for a second, then backed out. He didn't seem threatening, and after her initial fright, it was quite clear that he wasn't Clan. He didn't have the physique or menace of the Clan members, this was a boy who seemed to shrink into himself.

She made her way to Roisin's room. Knocking on her door, she shouted, "Roisin. Roisin! There's a strange boy in the house!"

Eventually there were noises of someone stirring, and the door opened. Roisin looked as if she'd only just got to sleep, and was far from happy at being woken up.

"He's on the computer – it looks like he's trying to smash the keyboard!" Sinter said.

"You're joking!" Roisin replied drowsily. "He can't still be here!"

The two of them walked through to the kitchen, and stood together watching the boy, his fingers flying over the keys.

"Minh!" Roisin finally called out. "Minh! Hey, what are you still doing here? You haven't been working all night, have you?"

The boy grunted by way of reply, motioning towards the screen.

"Minh, did you manage to sort out the bugs?" Roisin asked gently. Minh snorted again, this time in a way that seemed to say *that* was a task that a three-year-old could have managed. Roisin stood behind him, and placed one hand on his shoulder.

"Come on now, Minh, your ma said you could come

help me out, if you promised just to stay an hour or so. What have you been up to?"

Minh huffed pure sulkiness and stopped typing. He pressed a single button and the screen displayed a sequence of charts and neatly arranged numbers.

"My accounts!" gasped Roisin. "You've been through my accounts!"

"They were a mess," the boy retorted, in a manner that suggested he was surprised that anyone should mind him going through their personal accounts.

"What have you done? That . . . but . . ." Roisin was scrolling through the pages, incredulous. The figure at the bottom brought her up short.

"What have you done to it, Minh? There's no way we have that much money in the bank!"

Minh looked back at her with the kind of impatience a parent might show a clueless child. "You're just not very good at counting," he said without a hint of judgement, then turned back to the computer and closed the accounts, as his fingers again became a blur, this time creating vast swathes of binary code and incomprehensible computer language.

Roisin and Sinter quietly made themselves some coffee, and took it onto the steps outside.

"So what on earth was that all about?" Sinter began. "He scared me half to death!"

"Well, that's Minh," said Roisin. "But I guess you already know that. He's the son of one of my patients. When the computer broke down last week they offered to get him to come and see to it for me. He's . . . well, special, I guess."

"But he's clearly a nutter, you just let him wander round the house?"

"No, no, he's fine. He's just not very good with people. But he's obviously some kind of weird genius. I mean, in a few hours he's doubled our cash flow. And I wasn't expecting him to stay up all night!"

Later they made their way to work together, stopping at their favourite bakery to pick up fresh croissants.

Two streets away from the shelter, Sinter saw him.

"Roisin, please don't look, but we're being followed." Inevitably Roisin instantly looked around. "NO!" Sinter hissed, "I said don't look!"

"Oo, aren't you the jumpy one this mornin'!" Roisin joked. "And just who is following us then, Missy? Suppose it's some Bollywood leading man I never heard of!"

"This is serious, Roisin, he's behind us, thirty metres, grey hooded top, jeans, tall and slim."

"Blue eyes and blond hair no doubt," Roisin stopped and turned around, totally destroying any attempt at subterfuge. "Ah, what do you know? No hero after us I'm afraid, love." And then gesturing to an eighty-year-old man, stooped under a huge bundle of firewood, "Not unless you have a thing for much, much older men."

Sinter looked back down the street, aghast. She had been so certain, but there was no doubt: there was no one there. She really was losing it!

But as they walked on, in a nearby side street a tall young man lifted his sleeve to his hooded face, and seemed to talk into his cuff, before slinking off into the shadows.

The sinkhole gaped below his feet like the mouth of some gargantuan monster, stalactites around its rim forming mighty white fangs, the darkness of its gullet at once repelling him and calling him in. Coming up from inside was the stale smell of putrefaction, laced with sharp ammonia fumes from bat guano. Hagen had shown Saker a tangle of vines and old hemp rope that dropped into the abyss, and Saker had willingly taken them in his hands. He wasn't yet sure what he was being expected to prove, but was eager to show that he wasn't scared, and was prepared to make any sacrifice needed.

Hagen had spoken softly. "He who fights with monsters should look to it that he himself does not become a monster. And when you gaze long into an abyss, the abyss also gazes into you." The words were well chosen; the void seemed to be dragging Saker in, the horror of vertigo was singing in his ears, and he was filled with an almost hypnotic desire to throw himself over the edge to an unspeakable doom far below. When he tore his gaze away, Hagen was gone! Whatever task or challenge he was asking, Saker would have to face it alone. As he allowed his feet to swing free over the void, the full moon broke clear of a cloud, and washed the sinkhole with ghostly white light. Saker let out an involuntary gasp. The cave dropped down into the mountain as deep as a skyscraper is high. The empty air beneath his feet was seemingly infinite. He'd come too far to back out now though – the only way was into the abyss.

After about five minutes of descending, every sinew in his forearms seemed fit to rupture. Too late he remembered the advice he'd passed on to Sinter about climbing: "Always relax. The harder you hold on, the more energy you burn and the less strength you'll leave yourself." Already he felt at the brink of exhaustion, and in serious danger of not being able to maintain his hold on his lifeline. This was madness. If he fell and was smashed to death on the rocks below, the Penan would gain nothing. His mind made up, Saker started to climb back out. The effort took him by surprise. If descending had been physical, battling upwards against gravity on the thin ropes and slimy vines was impossible. He managed about three metres before accepting defeat. Forcing himself not to fight the lifeline, but to engage in a sort of controlled slide, he slithered into darkness.

It was a full fifteen minutes before his feet touched solid ground, by which time Saker's limbs were empty. He felt as if a pair of butterflies could have picked up each of his arms and flown away with them. Collapsing into soft sand, his face pressed into welcoming cool as he fought for breath. He was desperately thirsty, but had no water, and though his eyes were fighting to gain some point of reference in the black, he could see nothing at all. It was as though someone had pulled a velvet hood over his face, unseen dangers and foes lurked, invisible, in the gloom. Much as he battled against it, his heart was thumping in his throat, not the battle-ready surge of "the rush", but the paralysing hammer of fear. He groped around in increasing panic, fingers casting about for something familiar. They came upon a chilly object – round, coconut-sized, the top covered with straggly hair. Like a blind man seeking to see with his fingertips, he located sockets, then teeth. It was a human skull. As he battled to quell his fear, a giant centipede crawled out of the eye socket and over his hands. All reserve overwhelmed, he screamed, yelling to Hagen, to his Penan friends, to Sinter, but they were far away, and would never hear his screams.

You fight "the fear" in the same way you fight "the rush". Even though he could see nothing, Saker shut his eyes, and in his mind took himself away to his precious forest, to a high treetop looking out over the green ocean of the canopy. The thumping in his chest subsiding somewhat, he took stock. In his pocket were his fire-lighting scraper and flint, but he would have to find some fuel to use those. He could crawl around in the dark trying to feel

for wood, but there was too much risk of putting his hand
onto another of those highly venomous centipedes, not to
mention a snake or sharp rock. He looked up to the mouth
of the sinkhole above. It was just about possible to discern
what was the dark of the cave walls, and what was the
night sky beyond. Somehow that made it even worse; the
outside world was real, tangible, yet utterly unobtainable.
The sinkhole entrance was probably wide enough that
during the day a good deal of daylight would penetrate
to the floor. There was nothing for it, he would have to sit
exactly where he was until sunrise.

It was the longest night of his life. The sinkhole functioned
like a giant loudspeaker, amplifying every tiny sound. Every
distant drip sounded like a litre of blood spilling. Every
flutter of a bat wing became the flapping cape of a hidden
vampire just waiting for its moment to pounce. No matter
how much Saker told himself to stop being so pathetic, he
would twitch and curse in horror every time a cockroach
scampered over his feet. It felt as if the walls of the cave
were collapsing in on him, burying him under thousands
of silent tonnes of rock, sending his heart rate pounding
as if he'd just done three rounds on the punch bag.

The Clan demons appeared there in the darkness too.
Wolf towering over him, taunting him for his weakness.
The viperine shape of the boy Death Adder, his forked

tongue flickering over Saker's toes. And of course the Prophet in his blue samurai kimono, all-knowing, all-powerful, sneering at his protégé's descent into madness.

It was many hours before the bats' wings increased in frequency, as the colony started to return to the cave, their night's hunting done. Their wings teased the boy's face, making him squirm. However, the bats were the herald of the dawn. A dawn that rose on the tear-stained cheeks of a terrified child.

Finally, the sun broke over the trees above, and light started to make its way down the vertical walls of the cave. Saker stood, and held his hands up into the light, willing the golden beams to touch his fingertips and rescue him from the night. When they eventually did, he at last looked about and assessed his predicament. There was no escaping from the pit up the ropes; that was for sure. The ropes and vines were free-hanging for the full hundred or so metres of its depth. A gibbon or chimpanzee might manage it, but no human being could. Which brought things nicely to the human remains strewn about the cave floor. Not just a single skull, but several complete skeletons, grotesquely twisted. The tattered remnants of their clothes still lingered on their bones, they wore necklaces, and dreadlocks of hair still clung to their skulls. Their empty mouths seemed to be laughing at him. Hagen had sent him down here to certain death. There was no way out, no escape. He would die and rot here, and the Penan and Hagen would neatly avoid a tricky problem. The panic began to rise in his gullet again.

"Stop it!" he shouted, his voice echoing round the cavern.

The sunlight was by now reflecting down through the underworld, warming as it went. The bottom of the cave was a damp patchwork of soft sand and spiky limestone rocks, with spindly plants growing in between them. Water dripped constantly from the cave mouth, even now when there had been no rain for a day or so. It trickled off the bottom of the larger stalactites and percolated through the porous rock. Saker's throat was still parched after the efforts of the night before, and his thoughts immediately turned to slaking his thirst. Some of the plants had broad leaves, which turned like satellite dishes to capture the meagre sunlight that reached them when the sun was directly overhead. He tore a leaf off, and formed a crude bowl with it, then sat beneath a stalactite, allowing the trickle to fill his bowl with sweet water. It was no more than a mouthful at a time, but it was as if he was being physically recharged, the essential fluid bringing life back to his tattered muscles.

After drinking enough, he stood up, and noticed something that had until then been hidden. The white walls of the cave were stained with damp and mud, but in places the colours were much too deliberate to be natural.

As he drew closer, Saker gasped in wonder. The walls had been used as a stone canvas for breathtaking works of art. Perhaps the most common symbol was a human hand that had been used as a stencil, and paints of crimson ochre blown over the top of it. There were pictures of the mountains themselves, and all the creatures of the forest, some of them engraved in the rock with stone tools, others painted in organic dyes of purple, orange and yellow.

These were not the works of trapped, dying, condemned, desperate men. They were beautiful, contemplative and with purpose. The men who had made these works of art were working at leisure, not battling for a way to escape. It might as well have been written on the wall . . . there must be a way out of the cave.

Relief and excitement flooded through Saker like the warmth of hot chocolate on a winter's day. He was just about to turn away from the paintings, and start his search for the way out, when something drew him back to the scenes in front of him. It seemed there was a real journey, from the crude etchings on the left of the wall that looked utterly prehistoric, to much more developed works of art as he went further right. People had been making these paintings here for hundreds, possibly even thousands of years! His attention was caught by the simple, yet haunting representation of an orang utan, its lips pursed, eyes cast skywards as if in prayer. The orang utan's head merged seamlessly into the face of a Penan hunter, his dark features exactly the same. It was difficult to see where the ape finished and the man began, like ancient images of the two-headed god Janus, two sides of the same coin, mirror images joined in kinship. Saker knew that the very name, *orang utan*, means "man of the forest". They were a totem animal for the Penan, and sacred to them. This remarkable two-faced image was framed by forests, the home of the Penan, and the orange ape they shared it with.

As he continued walking the length of the dazzling tapestry, Saker saw figures and landscapes come to life. Penan gathering firewood, dancing through animated swaying trees, giving praise to the forest gods, always in equilibrium with their world. But then something changed. The scenes started to take on a nightmare quality; the forests were being destroyed. He saw starving babies, shrivelled menfolk in chains. And then he saw the figure of Lars, standing in front of the loggers' trucks. The vehicles seemed to possess evil grins, poised to leap on the tall Christ-like figure before them. The final image was the most chilling though, standing out starkly against all the others. There were no trees in the last scene, just towering buildings, blocky, as if drawn by a child. And cowering in the middle of them, sitting clasping his knees, was a tiny human figure. Alone, exposed, it was as if the buildings about him formed a prison cell and he had no way to escape. He gasped. The figure was Saker himself.

But then he looked again, more closely. Perhaps it wasn't him. Perhaps it was just a representation of any lost, lonely boy. The skill of the artist was such that anyone who viewed the image would surely see themselves in the vulnerable, terrified, imprisoned figure. "The abyss will look back into you," Saker mouthed.

It was a grim view of the future. This was why Lars had sent him down here. To get perspective. He was in the middle of something that was way bigger than the anger of one young man. Saker began to see. The Penan are guardians of a way of life that human beings have practised for several hundred thousand years. Since we came down from the trees perhaps six million years ago, human beings have always lived in the outdoors, surrounded by animals and wilderness. They are a part of us, he realised, and we are part of them. Saker nibbled on his lip as he scanned the pictures again. It was like the moment when one of those weird 3D stereogram pictures suddenly comes into focus. He saw that we need the Penan and the orang in ways we cannot understand. Without them, there will always be something missing, something we cannot put our finger on.

Saker thought of his life in the forest with the Clan, how it had left him happy in ways he couldn't even begin to describe. And how his life with the Penan had the same purity, how he wanted for nothing. It's only been within a few centuries or even decades that we've embraced technology, moved into big cities and cut our connections to the wild world. This is merely a blink of the eye in the grand scheme of things. The Penan, living in harmony with the world around them, hold a grand secret that modern man is wilfully destroying. The pictures of the cities now looked like concrete prisons. "We're destroying the places that make us human," Saker whispered.

He breathed out and looked once more into the soulful eyes of the orang utan. This was heavy.

6

It was almost too much to take in, and Saker still didn't know what Hagen wanted him to do with his newfound knowledge. All he knew was that the sinkhole felt like a tomb, and that he had to get out. He tried to put himself into the minds of the artists who had been here before him. The skeletons belonged to those who had not passed the test, and had failed to find a way out. Their forms were a challenge: fail to work out this riddle and Saker would end up like them. The artists, though, had worked here relaxed, easy, in the knowledge that leaving would be simple. Saker must be missing something obvious. Casting around, he noticed that the sinkhole was like a lopsided funnel. One side of the cave floor was lower than the other.

"Of course, all this water has to run away to somewhere; there must be a tunnel out of here!"

If the sinkhole formed a funnel, then the top of the spout must be at the lowest part of the cavern.

"Sorry, old timer," he apologised to one of the skeletons, as he broke off the femur – the upper leg, the longest bone in the body. He gathered as much of the dry old cloth of their clothes as he could, and wrapped it around the end of the leg bone. Taking his flint and scraper from his pocket, he chipped some highly flammable magnesium filings onto the cloth, then rasped the harsh file over a rock. Sparks flew onto the filings, and began to burn. The torch wouldn't last for long, so he needed to make the most of it.

At the deepest part of the cave was a tangle of boulders, the remnants of the mighty rockfall that had brought the roof down from way above them. Saker searched, looking for a hole that might lead down deeper into the mountain. Around his fingers blind cave crickets with enormous antennae many times their own body length sprang away, and long-legged centipedes scuttled. Then something caught his eye. One part of the rock was shiny, as if it had been polished. Polished by the movements of generations of men crawling along on their bellies. Saker dropped to his stomach, and pushed himself along the slippery rock, under a massive boulder ceiling. It was a tunnel! Again the faint light from the sinkhole above disappeared, and only the flickering light from the burning cloth lit the way. Instantly, claustrophobic panic threatened to overwhelm him. The night had affected him more than he had realised.

After a brief struggle, the tunnel narrowed, then turned a sharp corner. It would be snug even for a slightly built

Penan, but was practically impassable for Saker's muscular shoulders, especially as he was also trying to keep a flaming torch alight. Within seconds, it became impossible to go further. He was stuck. As he battled to free his shoulders the cloth dropped off the legbone torch to the rocky ground, flickered and burned out. Thousands of tonnes of solid stone above seemed about to collapse on his head, the walls crowded in . . .

"Nooo!"

This time the fear surged so quickly it drowned him, and he totally lost control, writhing, screaming like a caged creature. With one thrash to get free, he smashed his head on the rocky ceiling, and lay face first on the cool ground, unconscious.

When he came round, Saker could feel sticky blood gluing his face to the stone floor. Breathing out, he emptied the air from his lungs and became for a few seconds thin enough to slide through the squeeze that had him trapped. His shoulders scraped against the limestone, then his elbows, hips and knees. He jack-knifed his body, and popped through, sliding down a slight incline until he came to rest. The blackness was complete. He knew that nocturnal animals like owls and big cats have such well-developed eyes that they can draw in every scrap of available light, so can see pretty well in a midnight forest, but here in a cave with no light whatsoever, no animal on earth could see. Something ran over his hand. It was all he could do to suppress the panic. But it set his mind whirring. The long legs of the centipede, the antennae of the cave cricket – they were all adaptations to life in total darkness, highly sensitive organs that tap around in the pitch black serving as touch, taste and smell. Saker was going to have to learn how to perceive his world like a cave creature, and fast. Mammals, he figured, don't have antennae, but bats can echolocate, sending sonic clicks into the environment and then reading the signals as they bounce back. Saker tried it out, making a clicking sound with his tongue against the roof of his mouth. The echo came back instantly, and sounded dead, close. He put out his hand and felt solid stone right in front of his face. As echolocation went it was primitive, but it did work. What else? Most mammals have whiskers, long hairs on the face that are linked to highly sensitive bundles of nerve endings. Any stimulation of the whisker is transmitted straight back to the brain.

Saker held up his hand. The fine hairs on the back would have to function as crude whiskers. For what seemed like an age, he knelt poised, moving his hand around, senses on high alert. There! A slight tingling of the hairs – he was sure he felt it. A breeze; it had to be coming from the outside, a wind blowing into the tunnels and channelling through the cave system. He sniffed the ground and the air, like a bloodhound actively drawing scents into its nasal passages, where different molecules of odour can be assessed. It wasn't just the cloying dead air of the cavern any more – he could swear there was fresh humidity, the smell the forest has just before the rains. And perhaps the slight sharp tang of chlorophyll, like fresh-cut grass on an autumn morning. Saker turned his head to the left, but the scents and the breeze waned. He turned it to the right, and they shut off altogether. He tried the clicking sound again, but this time directed up above his head. The echo took almost a second to come back to him and sounded weak, distant, woolly. Tentatively he stood up, to find the ceiling was much higher here. And then the breeze hit him full in the face. Moving his head and clicking, Saker could almost see from the echoes where the walls were, and where there was empty space. Feeling around, another tunnel came to life under the gentle trace of his fingertips. Now it was unmistakable – his hair was gently agitating in the breeze, he could feel it on his cheeks, and his nostrils pulled by the strong scent of figs from a fruiting tree.

It was a battle against every instinct for him to crawl slowly down the tunnel, always sensitive to the invisible changes in the air. It would be disastrous to rush and miss a side shaft or crossroads, but the breeze and smells grew ever stronger. After so long in total blackness his eyes were playing tricks on him; was that an area of grey ahead? Was that moonlight? Now caution was abandoned in favour of an all-out scrabble down the tunnel, and out into the air. Tumbling head over heels from the tunnel down a grassy slope, he sucked in great lungfuls of sweet oxygen, grabbed handfuls of earth and pressed them into his face, and cried and cried with relief, the great weight of rock finally lifted from his world.

It took less than an hour to run back to the Penan village. His eyes were so fabulously adapted to the dark that he could see like an owl, and the sense of freedom was so overpowering that he could have sprinted for hours.

What he found at the temporary settlement brought him up short. It was empty. The fires had been extinguished and buried. There was no sign that anyone had been there for months. Saker walked disconsolately around what remained of the village. He had been through this whole hateful experience, and now the Penan had deserted him. He would have to find them again, whatever it took. The test had been passed; now he could be of real use. They may have deserted him, but the Penan and their orang utan brothers needed his help.. Searching the remnants of the buildings, he found the only belongings he'd brought with him from the outside world; a small rucksack with his identities, some money and the phone, which he hadn't even switched on in over a month. Perhaps he ought to return to Kuching city for a few days, regroup, get some good food and sleep in a bed for the first time in ages. Maybe it was about time he reconnected with the outside world. With that thought, he shouldered his pack, and ran off into the night.

Minh had become a familiar face at their house over the previous few days. Sinter tried repeatedly to engage him in conversation, but received a total lack of interest. First she thought he was shy, then rude, then finally she realised that he didn't see her at all. His world was the numbers and figures that rattled in front of him on the computer, people were like a foreign language. To begin with, Minh's mother was pleased to have him with them doing something useful. She changed her mind, though, when it became clear he was going well beyond just fixing a few bugs. It turned out that Minh had been in trouble with the police for computer hacking, and the only reason they'd let him stay out of prison was that they thought he was a bit simple. They'd released Minh on the promise that he didn't go anywhere near a computer, and here he was spending hours a day hooked up to the internet in Roisin's kitchen!

"I think he may have Asperger's Syndrome," Roisin had confided. "It's where you can't read other people's emotions. A lot of people who have it are called savants – you know, crazy geniuses at one thing, but not so good with human beings. They can remember a thousand telephone numbers, or pi to a hundred decimal places, but can't tell if someone's angry with them, or if they're hurting someone's feelings."

That seemed to make a lot of sense. Well, if he was a genius, reasoned Sinter, then they should make use of it! Early that evening after work, she sat down next to Minh, and asked if he wanted a cup of tea.

"Coke," he replied, then sipped at the drink in between flicking his hair out of his eyes.

"Minh, if I have someone's phone number, is it possible to find out where in the world they are?"

The boy stopped tapping but still looked forwards at the screen. "Not legally," he responded.

"Oh," Sinter replied, disappointed. It had seemed like the only way of finding where Saker was without actually forcing him to cross continents and come to find her, and in the process admitting that she was thinking about him.

But Minh hadn't finished. "But if you hack into the mobile service provider, and the phone is in use, you can triangulate the position to within a country, possibly a town." He resumed tapping, then spoke again. "If it's being used a lot you can pinpoint the phone to within a hundred metres."

"And you can do that?" asked Sinter, incredulous. It was the most words she'd heard him utter since she'd met him.

"Not legally," he responded.

In her room, Sinter fished in her rubbish bin, and retrieved the phone, picking off a bit of old chewing gum that had stuck to the screen. She scrolled down to the contact "taxi cabs" and looked at it long and hard, before putting the phone in her pocket. It wasn't dark outside, and she felt as if she needed to walk by the river to get a little perspective.

This time there was no doubting it. The Clan were here. The boy had been behind her at the first junction, and had followed her into the market. She stopped at a stall selling bits of cheap jewellery and tried on a plastic necklace, but as she admired it in the mirror, she turned it to reflect back the boy's face. He was pretending to be engrossed in a DVD stall. His eyes flicked to her. He was certainly no tourist. As soon as she moved away, the boy put his hands in his pockets and moved after her. This was not paranoia, it was real. There was a menace about his movements that chilled her blood. He was an identical build to Saker, but most of his face was still hidden by the hood, and she couldn't see it.

A plan was needed, and fast.

She turned around and pointed straight at him. "Thief!" she shouted in Vietnamese. "That boy stole one of your DVDs – I saw him!"

The stallholder at once leapt up indignantly and grabbed hold of the young man, who struggled to pull away, while trying to avoid making eye contact with Sinter. Engulfed in the chaos, Sinter ran. She dashed through the market, and out the other side into the crowded streets, eyes casting frantically for her next move. And then she saw the trap. Ahead on either side of the street were two more boys, unmistakably Clan, one stout and with next to no neck. Sinter instantly saw a killer whose Clan totem must surely be Bison or Buffalo. And on the other side of the street, a lithe, slinking viperine figure, definitely some kind of snake tattoo. Both wore the street uniform of the Clan; jeans and plain grey hooded top. They closed on her in a pincer movement, pushing the crowds firmly aside, no longer attempting to hide their identities. Sinter sprinted away, hailing a *tuktuk*. As it pulled up, she dived in one side, straight through and out the other, before ducking under a fruit stall, and through a doorway into a house.

She ran through the building, scattering children and protesting grandparents, out of the back door into the next alleyway. At one end she saw the silhouette of a hooded figure coming towards her; the boy from the market! His left hand was cupped backwards to disguise a weapon, probably a knife. She turned the opposite way and sprinted faster than she had ever run before. The alley opened into another street, and she nearly ran straight under a truck; the driver leant down on the horn. She yelped in fear, but didn't break stride, chasing down the pavement, pushing locals aside.

Despite the panic, her mind clicked back to what Saker had taught her. Sitting beside a stream in a Himalayan pine forest, where panic had seemed a million miles away, he'd taught her to recognise "the fear", and to have drills to beat it. "Know your location, know your escape route," he'd said. "Run through them over and over until they're second nature, so that your body takes over when your mind is clouded by adrenalin."

In those first few paranoid months in Ho Chi Minh, that's exactly what Sinter had done. While walking the streets, she was always mentally mapping them, remembering potential escape routes, continually planning for emergencies. She'd even run some of the streets with a stopwatch, timing different strategies. Once life had become happy this had begun to seem ridiculous and she'd stopped. Now it was time for that planning to pay off. Her brain clicked into status report mode.

"At least three pursuers. All bigger, stronger, faster, probably armed, and they're prepared for this. Keep running, and they'll hunt you down."

With that she danced through a patisserie that she knew had a back exit leading to the riverside. "What advantages do I have?"

It came to her instantly. "I know every millimetre of this city. They have only scoped the area of the ambush. So I need to get as far away as possible. Take them out of their kill zone, put them in unfamiliar territory."

With that she hurdled the fence by the river, and dropped to the path alongside the sloping concrete banks. Ahead of her was a broad bridge over the black, slimy water. Again the status report whirred in her head.

"Turn your weaknesses into strength. They're confident of their superiority, *that* is their weakness."

Sinter's tigress eyes found exactly what she was looking for – to one side of the bridge a tiny drainage tunnel that led down into the hell of the sewers.

"Being bigger and stronger isn't always an advantage . . ."

Just the thought of the place sent a shudder up her spine. She couldn't even bear to consider what lay down there.

"I need to go somewhere too small for them to follow."

Sinter slid down the concrete bank on her bottom as if it was a funfair slide, grazing her thighs even through her jeans. She barely registered the foul stench as she stomped through the polluted, oily waters. Without turning she could sense her pursuers hurtling down the slope, splashing into the water. They'd have her in seconds. The lead chaser's breath was hot on her neck as she reached the bridge and dived straight into the tiny drainage tunnel, crying out in disgust as the vile effluence splashed into her face. As she frantically crawled forwards into the darkness, a vice-like grip grabbed her foot. It could only be the boy Bison; the force was extraordinary. He pulled her effortlessly from the hole, like a fox might pull a rabbit from its burrow, or a blackbird tug a worm from a lawn. Sinter cried out in anger and fear, futilely, her fingernails clawed the tunnel walls. She kicked in fury towards an invisible foe. It couldn't end like this, face down in a sewer crying for mercy. But then her shoe popped off, planting her tormentor in the mud. Set free, she wriggled off down the tunnel, without a thought for the grazes on her knees and elbows, and the infections that might follow.

The hole burrowed beneath the bridge, then met a side tunnel that headed off to the right, and back under the city buildings. Behind her, the Clan boys were cursing and yelling as they struggled to cram themselves into the too-tiny tunnel. With the immediate threat gone, suddenly the full horror of her location hit her. The nausea of stinking heat, human waste, rats and cockroaches closed in, threatening to make her pass out. The vomit came, acid and unexpected. Coughing hot bile from her throat, she forced herself to concentrate, trying to reconstruct a virtual map of the city, and to visualise the buildings she was under. Shutting her eyes, she took herself away, up into the skies above, looking down on the city with a falcon's-eye view, plotting her subterranean route.

Returning to Roisin's house or to the shelter was out of the question. The Clan would be expecting that, and would be waiting. Sinter had, however, planned for this eventuality from her first few days in the city. In one of the bars where she'd first taught English, behind the jars of pickled snake whisky, she'd hidden a cigar box full of money in four currencies. There was also a fresh passport and the precious locket her mother had given her.

No clean clothes though, she thought ruefully. But what else did she have? A crazy thought popped up in her mind. Yes! Sinter stopped crawling, and reached into her pocket. Saker's mobile phone. This was surely the exact situation he had been talking about. No time for pride now. Trying to keep her fingers from trembling, she scrolled down the contacts to "taxi cabs".

"Send text message," she said out loud. The message screen popped up, and she started to type, entering latitude and longitude co-ordinates she'd imprinted into her brain. She pressed "Send". The status bar popped up, and tried to send the message. Then stopped dead. There wasn't enough reception.

"No, no! Come on!" she shouted at the phone, but it was no use; her concrete prison was blocking any signal.

Crawling on through the darkness, Sinter became aware of pale shafts of light creeping down. Ahead was one of the countless places where the pavement above had collapsed. Escape! Fighting back tears, she pulled herself up into dusk. She was free! All around her, the city folk stared with a mixture of disgust and interest at the shoeless girl dripping in unspeakable grime, but she didn't care –

anything to be out of that horrific place. Turning in the direction of the bar and her lifeline, she took flight.

Almost instantly she ran straight into a solid figure. Gasping at the lock of his grasp on her arm, she looked up into a familiar face. Almost shaved hair, dark brows and brooding looks, ice-blue eyes and broad shoulders that moved easily above a narrow waist.

"Wolf!"

A sharp needle punctured her jeans and stabbed into her backside. Even if she could have fought free of his iron grasp, before she could draw another breath the world started to fog. She sensed the other Clan members running up behind, felt herself falling into the arms of the boy she'd christened Bison, felt the darkness close, and then . . . nothing.

As the boys dragged her away, from her back pocket came two beeps from her phone. A sound that confirmed a text message had been sent.

8

Upon waking Sinter sprang up and instantly struggled to get free from the arms of Bison and Wolf, but found herself alone. She was lying in a bed in a long dormitory, with rows of empty beds side by side as far as she could see. Ceiling fans whirred lazily overhead, casting long moving shadows across the walls. Whatever sedative Wolf had injected her with had stolen time; she had no sense of how long she might have been unconscious. It might have been minutes, but could have been weeks. It was night, and through the high windows the moon cast a blue light around her massive cell. Alongside her bed were numerous medical machines, some of which were attached to her with sticky pads. A long tube ran down and into a vein in the back of her hand. Wincing, Sinter pulled the needle out, threw her bedclothes off, and slid out of bed. Her bare feet touched cool concrete, and a flimsy hospital nightdress flapped around her knees. Running the length of the room in between the beds, she came to a door. She tried the handle. Nothing. It was locked. All caution gone, she yanked and pulled on the door, then smashed it with her fists. There was nothing but the dull echo of her screams and pounding, resounding in long empty corridors beyond.

"A shame you removed that needle," a voice addressed her calmly. Sinter started, and turned to look into the shadows.

"We'll have to put in another, and after a while the veins start to pucker, like a slug dusted with salt." The voice took extraordinary relish in the image, tasting the sounds of each word like honey. Then Sinter saw him. In the corner sat a man wearing the loose-fitting light blue robe of a Japanese samurai, darker blue trousers beneath. Shadows across his face accentuated a strong, sharp nose and fierce features, his eyes black hollows in the night light. He ran a hand over his scalp, seeming to revel in the sensation of scratching his clipped white hair.

"And you've got more than enough to worry about with all the . . . *medicines* we've had to give you." Again, the word "medicines" was given special emphasis on his lips.

"You should be quite proud of yourself. You're rather unusually strong . . . robust. Many of my boys wouldn't have been able to take all the . . . *treatment* you've undergone."

"Perhaps I was wrong to keep my business so strictly . . . male only."

Sinter exploded on him with a fire and fury that came

from the bottom of her gut. Her fingernails went for those shrunken eyes, the exposed claws of an uncaged tigress. The figure stood abruptly, his chair sliding cleanly back across the floor and clattering into the wall. His movement was so slight and fast it was barely perceptible, but nonetheless her feet were swept up to where her head should have been, and her body hit the concrete floor, driving the air from her lungs. As she lay battling to breathe, the figure in blue walked back to his chair, picked it up and walked back to her side. He placed it close and sat.

"What are we to do with you, little tigress?" he asked in mock exasperation. "You and our mutual renegade friend have caused me no end of . . ." he breathed in, searching for the word that would taste best on his papery lips. "*Consternation*. Sleepless nights, wasted thoughts, wasted efforts. The evenings I've spent staring into dancing flames and wished you both harm. And now here we both are."

Sinter choked through her pain, "So sorry to have inconvenienced you."

The man stood, and swung his chair so it pinned Sinter down, a bar right across her throat. "You will learn to sheathe those claws, little tigress. You will learn many things, whether you like it or not. I'm going to enjoy having a new . . . *pupil*. And one who'll be so . . . very . . . *willing*." With that his lips flipped back to reveal a freakishly perfect set of white teeth. It was more like the warning teeth-flash of a baboon or chimpanzee than the laughter of a man. This time Sinter moved too quickly for him, her fingernails raking his exposed leg, tearing deep into the flesh. He flinched in pain and surprise, then pressed the bar of the chair down on her throat. Sinter fought bravely, clawing at the air, battling against the red cloud that was flooding her brain, but the lack of oxygen began to tell within mere seconds, and darkness overcame her again.

Next time Sinter came round, it was as if in a sick nightmare. She was looking out of her own eyes, but imprisoned within her body. Her hands were moving in front of her, but she couldn't control them. She tried to shake it off, tried to scream, but her body was no longer under her control. A voice was whispering in her ear.

"You are my special weapon, little tigress. And now your claws will only be unsheathed when I require it." She turned and looked at the face pressed too close to hers. Within the sunken sockets his eyes were the blue of glacial ice, intoxicating, hypnotic. She knew who he was. Saker had not talked enough about his childhood with the Clan, mostly because he didn't seem to understand it himself. However, he had occasionally mentioned the Prophet. He was the Clan's chief teacher, a menacing presence who ruled the boys through fear. Despite Saker's bravado, she could tell that it was difficult for him even to mention the

Prophet's name. It was clear he was a man of whom she should be very frightened, and he seemed to have her under some kind of spell.

The Prophet continued, "He is a traitor to the cause. I know he helped you escape the fortress, helped you set loose my . . . *consignment*." A lick of the lips, indescribably sinister. "I tried to bring him back into the fold, but he is not himself; I fear he never will be. Will you solve this little problem for me?"

Sinter stuttered through her tears, "No, no, I won't." Every word was a battle. "You don't control me," she said.

"Oh, but I do."

It was then that she became aware of someone else in the room with them. Kneeling on the floor in front of her, clad in a simple cotton tunic and jeans, was Saker. Hands tied behind his back, head bowed, perhaps unconscious.

"You know what you have to do," the Prophet said.

She sobbed, trying to speak to her friend, desperate to force her hands to obey commands, wanting to stop them picking up the knife that lay on a metal table before her. One of her sobs brought him round, and his eyes met hers. His face was beaten and bloodied, but it was not Saker. It was Polecat. She saw the brief flicker of recognition in his eyes, and then horror at the blade in her hands. It was a *tanto*, the short sword that samurai warriors used to wield in ceremonial suicides, slicing open their own bellies in ritual disembowelment.

Polecat was Clan. He had been part of the team that

had kidnapped Sinter. However, the young boy's will had not been strong. When he was faced with the reality of the Clan, of the evils they were perpetrating against powerful totem animals like tigers, Polecat had betrayed his masters. He had helped Saker and Sinter set the captive tigers free, and aided their escape from a citadel in the Himalayas. While Saker and Sinter ran, Polecat had returned to the Clan, hoping his treachery would go unnoticed. Clearly this had not happened.

"He has nothing now," the ice-eyed figure taunted. "He cannot be Clan, cannot be what he once was. But we can't let him return to the wild. Not after such . . . treachery." In his mouth the word sounded like candy, like a sticky toffee apple.

"There can only be one punishment. Treason still carries the death penalty in so many places around the world. And a dog that bites his master must be . . . put to sleep." As if taking on the role, Polecat was starting to whimper like a puppy. He could no longer look Sinter in the eye. She, for her part, was battling to drop the knife, fighting against the insidious vines that were growing through her sinews, controlling her every movement. Whatever drugs they had flooded her veins with had total hold. She simply didn't have the strength to fight it.

"Do it, little tigress. One less tiger-killer in the world. One less Clan member, one you'll never have to run from again. Cut his throat, you will be showing mercy , releasing him . . . do it. DO IT!"

She was powerless. Walking forwards like a marionette, with every movement choreographed by an unseen puppeteer, she took a scruff of Polecat's hair in her fist and drew his head back, looking into his terrified eyes. The blade touched the exposed white skin of his throat and, as tears rolled down her cheeks, Sinter managed to choke out a few words. "I'm so, so sorry."

9

Mobile phone masts had been springing up even in Borneo, and Saker hadn't even got to the outskirts of Kuching city before the signal became active, and a message from Sinter came through. As he looked at the simple string of numbers she had sent, a chill flooded through his bloodstream. There was no message, as he had instructed, just the co-ordinates of where he could find her. Sinter was too proud to send for help unless she was in mortal danger. Thoughts of Hagen, orang utans, the Penan and the forests of Borneo would have to wait.

Saker had suddenly experienced a sensation he had never felt before. A deep churning in his stomach, accompanied by horrible visions of Sinter being captured, screaming for help and in pain. The images were unbearable, all he wanted to do was get to where she was and make it all stop. This sense of protectiveness towards her, of wanting to take her pain away, even to sacrifice himself to protect her . . . it was all new. All he knew was that if he didn't get to Sinter soon, then he would never see her again.

The quickest route would have been to buy a plane ticket from Borneo to Ho Chi Minh, but he wasn't sufficiently confident of his fake ID to risk international customs. If the Clan had his passport flagged up on their systems, he would step off the plane into the arms of waiting officials. The more times he flew, the greater the risks. Also, though he could barely admit it to himself, after his ordeal in the cave the idea of being trapped inside a metal tube flying high over the ocean made him feel sick. Instead, Saker made his way to Kuching city port. Giant wooden schooners sat in the harbour, with high masts and sails made of hemp cloth. The boats had barely changed in hundreds of years, and were still transporting logs around Asia, and spices from the islands further to the east. There were also the much smaller boats of the Bajau people, gypsies who spent their entire lives at sea. Families of ten inhabited small, brightly coloured wooden boats perhaps eight metres long. They lived off whatever the oceans could provide, and rarely came to shore. More importantly, though, for Saker's needs, they sailed where they pleased, had no passports and paid no heed to international borders. If he could get passage with a Bajau family, he'd be able to cross the continent without anyone ever knowing. All he needed was to find one that was sailing north, across the South China Sea to Vietnam.

After a full day wandering along the quay and quizzing every boat captain, he found a family who were heading in the right direction and were willing to take him along for a few hundred dollars. The Bajau have little use for money, except to pay for fuel for their boats. Otherwise, everything they need, the seas provides. Early in the morning and late afternoon they sat out on the roof, singing, chatting and playing cards. They don't seem to mind the acrid smell from the stacks of salted fish and stingrays drying there in the fierce equatorial sun. When the fish is fully dried out it'll keep for months, though Saker could never force himself to try eating any of it. Aside from those cool parts of the day, it was simply too hot to be on the roof, so the rest of the day was spent shaded in the cramped interior of the boat. It was a noisy, chaotic place to be, with babies wailing as they bounced in little hammocks sprung with bicycle inner tubes. Older children played with homemade kites or carved toy boats out of balsa wood, while the adults caught fish and freedived for shellfish. They swam like dolphins, holding their breath for inhuman lengths of time, and seemed to know at birth which fish are good to eat and which are poisonous. The Bajau nomads had no great agenda, wandering where the fishing is good, and with no need to rush at anything, so Saker had to pay them extra to leave on the next tide.

The Bajau were totally at ease on the open sea crossing, but Saker was a child of the trees and the open sky. It was an unpleasant surprise to find he got horribly seasick, and spent most of the days staring at the horizon, or vomiting noisily over the side. I'm a jungle bunny, not a wave rider, he thought to himself miserably as he pressed his face to the wooden deck, willing the world to stop going up and down. The young children looked at him in astonishment, they'd been lullabied by waves since they were born, and couldn't understand how it could make him so ill. The elders looked at him with pity, and would give him chunks of raw ginger root to chew on. It was supposed to help with the nausea, but it didn't. At times, it got so bad that he ignored the sunburn, and would lie up on the top deck with the waves lashing over him, then let the salt dry in the sun, forming a white crust over his skin. At night the whole family would curl up inside the cabin, huddled together from the damp sea wind. Saker was always crammed next to the grandfather, who usually had his bony knee between Saker's shoulder blades, and snored like an ancient lawnmower. It was a special kind of hell.

Fortunately though, there were no storms, and the winds and tides were favourable, so ten days later, they sailed up the estuary of the mighty Mekong river and finally saw their first dry land since leaving Borneo. Rice paddies ran down to the water on either side, then the sprawl of the city itself began. It took all Saker's restraint not to leap overboard and swim for land.

He took his leave of the Bajau at a dock in the centre of the city. The family watched in silence as the green-faced young man went down on his knees on the concrete pavement as if thanking some land god, almost weeping with the joy of being free from the sea. However, though the crossing had been vile, his plan had worked. They had made their way into Vietnam completely under the radar, and never had to show any identification or have any contact with the authorities. Whoever had captured Sinter would have no idea he was coming, and that at least was a small advantage.

Saker had been walking the streets for several hours before his whole world stopped going up and down and the seasickness was truly gone. But there was too much to do. He headed to an internet cafe to narrow down the co-ordinates that Sinter had sent him. A government-run website contained maps that led him to a district number in the heart of the city sprawl, but that would not be precise enough. Saker racked his brains. Where would she go? What would she do? He trawled his memory, trying to put himself in her shoes. Surely it would have to be something to do with medicine? It took a few hours of searches. First of all he scanned to try and find a hospital within the radius of Sinter's lat and longs, but there was nothing nearby. Then he started trying smaller medical centres and charities. Eventually he came across a website showing the privately-run refuge "The Ho Chi Minh Refuge". There was a photo of a red-haired lady he would soon come to know as Roisin, receiving a present of a basket of fruit from a beaming old lady. He would have skipped straight past the photo but something caught his attention; there in the background, trying to blend with the scenery, was a young girl in Western clothes. Saker zoomed in. Her amber eyes were transfixing, even in the low-res internet photograph. It was Sinter. There was a little leap in his chest as he saw his friend's face for the first time in months. He searched some more but couldn't find anything else, and that one photo gave nothing away. He couldn't tell if she was happy or healthy, if she was there against her will or living out her dreams. "But I'll be able to ask her that myself soon enough," he told himself. Saker's last move before leaving the cafe was to use Google Earth to zoom in on the streets around the centre. He made printouts of the buildings, the rooftops, and marked up the copies with all the possible escape routes. He didn't know what he would be facing, but could not be too prepared.

Saker shouldered his bag and headed into the city swelter. It was all too tempting to blunder in straight away, but he knew that would be a mistake. For whatever reason Sinter had summoned him, there must be danger lurking. Someone would be watching. He needed to be smart, and that meant being patient.

So Saker went shopping. He planned his destinations and purchases with military precision, and finally as night fell, made his way through the backstreets towards the centre. He climbed up onto the flat roof of a building that offered a fine panoramic view of the city, and most importantly down to the alleyway to the centre. Any normal evening, the thick polluted air and whine of mopeds would have kept him awake, but he was exhausted, and dropped off easily into deep sleep.

Baking sun woke him not long after dawn. Saker rolled over to his rucksack, taking care to keep his profile low and not create a silhouette against the sky. From his bag he took out the kind of spotting scope that is normally attached to a sniper's rifle, and scanned the streets, cupping one hand over the front lens to avoid sun glinting off the glass and giving away his position. The streets were still quiet. It was a full hour before he spied Roisin arriving, tiptoeing down the boardwalks, greeting the street hawkers selling their wares and those already queuing, before lifting the screens and opening up.

All day he waited, the sun tanning his hide and bleaching his bones, but Sinter never appeared. And though he trained his spotting scope on every bit of concrete, there were no characters that stood out, nobody else was watching Roisin. Finally, sunburned, patience worn thin, he saw Roisin emerge and drop the shutters. Her day was done and she was heading home. Saker packed his things, and scrambled down the side of the building. On the ground, he pulled a cap over his eyes, and a bandanna up to obscure his lower face. Many people on the streets wore face masks to strain pollution out of the air, so it shouldn't mark him out as unusual. He fell in behind Roisin, far enough back that she wouldn't see him and he could watch the people who might be watching her.

They zigzagged down the streets, Saker's eyes always busy, flicking around analysing everything he saw. The printout was in his hands, and he followed their route closely. After fifteen minutes she arrived at her house, put her key in the lock and went inside. Saker dropped back, slinking into the shadows. Taking out his scope, he surveyed the area, finally settling on the door of the house. He took the number and the road name, and pulled his phone from his pocket. Scribbled on the back of the printout were a list of numbers. He called one and stood back to wait. Twenty minutes later, a pizza delivery moped arrived. The driver got off, took a pizza from the carry-box and walked up and rang the doorbell. Saker watched through the scope with interest as Roisin answered the door. She looked confused, and was clearly telling the pizza delivery boy that she hadn't ordered anything. They had a short and obviously rude argument, but Saker couldn't see signs of anyone inside the house, or around on the streets watching. It seemed the coast was clear.

He decided to wait just another half an hour for safety. By now it was dark again, and Saker hadn't eaten in twenty-four hours. Hunger was gnawing his belly, but it would have to wait. He put his hands in his pockets and walked across the street and knocked on the door. Roisin opened it. She looked into Saker's face, and gasped with recognition. "You shouldn't have come here," she said, her voice thick with fear.

"Why not?" replied Saker.

"Because we knew you would," said a voice inside the house. Then Wolf stepped into the hallway.

Saker turned to run, but in the street opposite saw a figure move into the pool of light under a streetlamp. As he stood frozen, a silhouetted Clan member stepped from the dark into every beam down the street. There would be no escape this time.

10

Had she imagined it? Could the nightmare of the previous night have been real? As the fog lifted from her waking mind, Sinter found herself back in the long dorm with the blue light, and the fans helicoptering above. The needle had been replaced in the back of her hand, but now she was bound to the bed, broad straps holding her firmly in place. She struggled long enough to know it was futile, then slumped back into place.

"Rest, little tigress, you have a very busy day ahead." It was the papery voice again. Sinter twisted to try and look into his eyes, but the straps didn't allow it.

"Last night was just a rehearsal, but your performance was . . . *exquisite.*"

"What have you given me?" Sinter screamed. "What are you doing to me?"

The Prophet moved into her line of sight, placing his

hand on her forehead in a paternal gesture that could have been caring, so seemed even more repellent. "I am giving you a great honour, tigress – you should be very proud. I am breaking all the rules for you. You will be the first ever girl to join us."

Sinter was appalled. "I'd rather die here. Your little boys' club is sick."

"Mine?" The Prophet questioned as if flattered. "Child, the Clan has been in place for far longer than I have been alive."

She heard him pulling up a chair alongside her and sitting. It was as if he was taking a comfy chair to tell her a bedtime story.

"Over two centuries ago the Clan began as the private army of the Romanian royal family. The princes were keen for power, but they needed to overthrow their parents. Obviously as men of royal blood, they didn't want to dirty their own hands. The palace guard were loyal to the king and queen, and other soldiers simply couldn't be counted on. But the princes were patient. They reasoned that if young boys were taken from their families when they were just babies, they became unusually . . . *pliable*."

"You mean easily brainwashed?"

"You can call it that if you wish." He seemed perfectly comfortable with that. "An egg that is taken from the nest, upon hatching will imprint on the first thing it sees. An ostrich chick can believe its mother is a humble hen, and will follow it for life, even when it could crush its parent beneath its toes." He contemplated his own imagery with pleasure.

"Their first experiments met with great success. They trained a small group of boys to levels of loyalty that were quite . . . remarkable. After less than a decade of training, the first of the Clan tore the reigning monarchs into pieces like wild dogs." He paused as if remembering the scene, which Sinter noted had happened two centuries before the Prophet had been born.

"After their first initiates had removed the king and queen from the throne, the princes faced a rebellion. The people after all were in mourning, they remained loyal to the dead king and rumours were growing of . . . *foul play*. The princes used their new young regiment to spread terror and chaos among their subjects. Those who led the rebellion were found dead in their beds. Their wounds were horrible – it was as if they had been rent apart by wild beasts. Next the *cleansing* spread to the wives of the rebels, their children, people they lived next door to or played cards with. The Clan left no traces behind. Those who opposed the princes would always be looking over their shoulder. Terror became a way of life." The next lines were delivered with pride. "Those first heroes of the Clan, they showed an unusual talent for . . . *cruelty*. Eventually they didn't have to kill any more. Fear was enough to keep things in order."

All Sinter knew of the history of Romania was the violent reign of Vlad the Impaler, the dictator who had killed tens of thousands of his own kind as well as his enemies, impaling them on great wooden stakes. The historical figure had given rise to the legend of Count Dracula. Reality became myth became legend. Was this all this was? Perhaps the Prophet was trying to fill her with fear, make her easier to manipulate. There was no way she'd let that happen!

"So you think you're descended from royalty? You think you're part of some kind of noble tradition? That's pathetic. You're just trying to justify what you're doing, to convince yourself that there's some kind of twisted history to it."

"Not at all," he countered. "That is what the Clan *was*. What it is now is something else entirely. I'm a businessman."

"Poachers for hire?" snapped Sinter. "Dirty criminals with no loyalty to anyone, on offer to the highest bidder?"

"That's one way of looking at it. Rather an ungracious way, though. Another would be that we are an independent organisation with no ties to anyone, with contacts in every government around the world," he responded coolly. "And anyone who isn't already in my pocket, all I have to do is send my boys to stop by late one night. They are soon my friends. Or . . . we take measures to ensure they are not a problem."

"So you steal children from their families? Turn them into criminals? You must be so proud! I guess it's too tough to work on someone your own age," Sinter sneered.

"But it must be children, don't you see?" The Prophet

was grinning now, clearly warming to his task and eager to enlighten Sinter.

"A modern soldier doesn't even start training till he is eighteen years old. All of the best learning years are already behind him, wasted. A national army is trained in their thousands, and with meagre resources. Give me one child at birth, let me have him for every hour of his waking life, with the best training methods that both nature and science can provide, and I will create an assassin who is worth ten professional soldiers . . . a hundred!" He was animated now, like a mad preacher, spitting fire and brimstone. "I have created an army of no more than a handful of young men, who can bring down a nation. And you will be a part of it."

Sinter shuddered. She knew that this could never be so, but she also knew that whatever the clear liquid was that was dripping into her veins, it had a horrid control over her.

"You didn't answer my question. What are you giving me?"

The Prophet smiled. "A little bit of this, a little bit of that. In the past, armies have been far more open to experimenting with . . . *magic potions* . . . then morality started to get in the way." He said the word "morality" as if it was the dirtiest word in the world.

"So you haven't got what it takes to control babies by yourself – you have to use drugs?" She was taunting him now.

"I am leading the next generation of the Clan," he retorted with pride. "Under my leadership the Clan has become more powerful, more wealthy than my predecessors could ever have dreamed. Why not take advantage of the benefits of the modern world? Especially in challenging cases . . . like your own."

Sinter so wanted to lash out at him, but knew that watching her struggling against the bonds would give the Prophet pleasure. Instead she continued to search for a weakness in him. If the Clan and its way had become his religion, then anything said against it would seem like heresy.

"So you flounce around in your robes, like some messiah, stringing kids out on drugs and turning them into petty thieves?"

"There is nothing petty about the deeds we do," he responded. "And the society we work outside of, do you really believe it is so perfect? A society where a wealthy person spends more on their car than an entire poor village would need to live for a decade? Where we feel free to pump the air full of poisons the people then have to breathe, and taint the water they drink with human effluence? Where someone can drink a glass of champagne that costs more than a medicine that would stop a man a mile away dying from vile diseases? A society that encourages big businesses to ravage the earth for every one of its resources? There are no innocents left, little tigress."

"But that's exactly what *you're* doing!" she cried out. "You make out like you're men of the forest, but you'll quite happily kill everything that's in it if it makes you money."

"That is the way of the predator. Kill or be killed. That is nature. You have much to learn."

That was not true. Sinter knew in her heart it wasn't true. Subconsciously she rubbed her lower leg with her foot, stroking the monochrome tiger tattoo she so treasured. Saker had painstakingly given her the mark as a badge of honour, a sign not just of her ferocity, but of her cunning, her courage, her loyalty and her capacity to lay her life on the line. These were the traits of the tiger, and of all predators. Even a female crocodile will sacrifice her life to protect her eggs or her hatchlings. There was far more to being the most powerful than being a mindless killer, and Sinter knew it.

She spoke with certainty. "All this cloak and dagger secret stuff is just rubbish; talk all you want, but you KNOW this is all wrong."

"Secrecy has many benefits. When the Clan began, we had to keep ourselves from view. It wouldn't do to have the peasants knowing their missing boys had been . . . *adopted* by royalty. And then when they became a private army, the secret became even more powerful. People talk, secrets breed fear, twisted truths become folklore. To some the Clan were vengeful spirits, silent trolls who took their newborn boys by night. To others they were an invisible pack of wild animals that slaughtered the enemies of the state. The people believed they were not human, and could not be killed or stopped. Terror is a tool to keep the little man in his place."

Sinter's mind was struggling to keep up with all that she was hearing. So the Clan had begun as a secret army? But in order to keep the people frightened, their deeds would have to be public, even if the Clan themselves were not.

"No one is frightened of you now. Nobody has even heard of you."

"Yes they have. We have provided services all over the planet. Everyone is familiar with our work; they just don't know it."

Sinter's imagination started sparking with crazy images. She was no stranger to conspiracy theories; if the Prophet was serious then there was no end to past crimes the Clan could be culpable of. Evil went by many names around the world. Some of the biggest moments in history – wars, invasions, toppling of governments – had all been triggered by important incidents that could easily have been the work of a small powerful organisation. But no, that was madness! She had no proof the Clan had any power at all. Except for the fact that they had found her. How much influence would it have taken just to locate her here in Vietnam? And as for control, she only had to think of Polecat, looking up at her with pleading eyes . . . she shuddered with horror, then shook her head; it couldn't be true. They were just a bunch of young boys, who had spectacularly botched the only operation she knew for a fact they'd been involved in. They couldn't possibly be all that the Prophet was claiming. He was just some loony who thought he was, well, a prophet!

"So how do you choose which babies to abduct then?" Sinter asked.

The Prophet leapt back to his feet, and stood over her. He wasn't angry though – he was filled with fervour. "That's the most elegant part of the whole story. I have found the finest solution to that problem!" Sinter turned her head to look into his icy eyes. She had never heard anyone sound so impassioned, he was clearly desperate to tell her something, but before he could unleash his last bombshell, he was cut short by another voice shouting from the far end of the room.

"We've got him!" a Clan boy yelled, his tones cloyed as if he had just finished a big slice of cake. Sinter fancied it must be Bison. At first the excitement went out of the Prophet's eyes, and she thought he would unleash fury on the boy for interrupting, but then a new coldness came over him.

"How touching – he came back for you. I am clearly not the only one who recognises you are special."

"Saker?" she gasped. The Prophet nodded.

"So now you know, nobody is going to save you."

Sinter's mind whirled like the rickety fans above her. There had always been hope, the merest possibility that Saker would come to her aid, but instead she had led him straight into a trap. And while the Prophet clearly wanted her alive, she had no doubt that he would want final justice for Saker. She had to think fast.

"So now you have him, you don't need me any more," she said.

The Prophet actually laughed out loud. "I have to admit that originally he was my first priority. We needed to seek *retribution* . . . he simply couldn't be wandering the world with a head full of secrets." The Prophet scratched his white hair again. "But I've come to realise a few things in our short chats. I was looking for my prize in the wrong place." He stroked her cheek with the back of his hand. Sinter recoiled as if a cockroach had slithered over her skin.

"One of the great triumphs of the Clan is that no one suspects a child to be capable of anything. The public automatically underestimates a young face, treats them like morons, subhuman beings. As you have seen, this is utterly misguided. With you it will be even more so. They will see a beautiful young girl of high-caste Indian heritage and believe that all you are capable of thinking about is flowers and marriage and, as we both know, that is pure nonsense. You have already proved you can wield a knife. Special Forces soldiers are taught that if they encounter a room full of armed terrorists, they should focus on the female soldiers first. Girls have a *ruthlessness* . . . pure cold determination when they are protecting their own. I am ashamed at myself for taking so long to realise this."

"But I'll never work for you. You can't keep me hooked up to this for the rest of my life!"

"I won't have to," he cut her short. "Because now I have something precious to you." With that, he slashed her bonds, and Sinter rolled out of the bed and onto the cold concrete floor. "And now I have the means to control *everything* you do."

11

Everything in Roisin's world had been turned upside down in the space of a few days. It was clear that Sinter was hiding a dark secret, but then all young runaways had something murky in their past. Roisin hadn't pushed her, figuring that Sinter would open up when she was ready. Besides, the girl was a good soul, with a keen mind and a way with people that made her a natural healer. Roisin had obviously wondered what the secret was, but had never believed Sinter was actually being followed. When she went missing though, it was immediately clear that something big was wrong. Nothing had been taken from the apartment, and she hadn't left a note. Twenty-four hours after her disappearance, Roisin went to the police and tried to file a missing persons report. They replied that Sinter's embassy would have to be notified. That was when Roisin realised that she didn't even know where her friend came from. With no passport, ID, or even a second name it was impossible. Roisin approached the Indian, Bangladeshi and Pakistani embassies, but none of them were aware of anyone called Sinter being in Vietnam.

That was when it occurred to Roisin to go to Minh. She asked him as he was about to pull another all-nighter at their computer. In the dark his face was illuminated by the screen, lines of code flickering across his features.

"Minh," she offered. Then something about his indifference and her own nervousness made her shout, "MINH!" There was still no response. She took a deep breath and tried again. "Minh, I have something I need you to do." His fingers didn't stop tapping. "You're right, it's probably too hard – I shouldn't even have thought of you." His fingers stopped.

"I am making a multi-headed hydra worm," he said. "There are approximately two hundred thousand lines of code to write. I am quite busy."

"I understand that, Minh, but there is a real problem. Sinter has gone missing. I can't find her . . . actually I can't even find out who she is." With this Roisin cracked, and let out a short sob. "She's in trouble."

Minh finally turned and looked at her. He regarded her tears with a confused expression. "You want me to find your housemate?"

"Yes! But it's not spying on her or anything – I just want to find her. She's missing, in danger . . . can you help?"

Minh nibbled at his lip. "But a five-year-old could do that. You just need to do a simple search."

"OK then," said Roisin. "But I'll need my computer back for a few days."

Minh's reaction was instant – he actually took the keyboard in his arms as if Roisin might take it from him.

"No! No, I'll do it. I just need to finish the next class in the firewall-breaching protocol."

With that, Roisin knelt down next to the power outlet as if to turn the computer off at the mains. "No, Minh, you will do this for me NOW, or you will find somewhere else to do your illegal . . . stuff."

Minh sighed, then tapped a key. The binary disappeared, and with another tap an internet search engine appeared. His fingers started to fly over the keys.

Next morning, Roisin woke to the noise of typing. She found Minh crouched over the keyboard, brow furrowed, purple sagging beneath his eyes, face clammy with sweat. He clearly hadn't stopped all night.

"So have you found anything?"

He stopped, and blew out through pursed lips.

"Yes . . . and no. I found reference to a girl called Sinter who went missing in Assam in India last year. There was a thread on a chatroom that had been discussing it. But it was deleted, and the whole thread was encrypted. As soon as I tried to crack it, they launched a worm on me."

Roisin's quizzical expression showed that Minh might as well have been talking in a foreign language.

"It's a trace, searching for our ISP, basically a couple of hundred digital bloodhounds tracking the web searching for me. I spent four hours evading it. All online newspaper reports referring to Sinter have been digitally excised."

Roisin considered asking what this meant, but figured it was tech-speak for them having been deleted. She had never heard Minh talk this much, and decided it was best not to interrupt him.

"And not just excised, but even the mirror image of them on the actual discs has been hidden – high-duty protection stuff. But it gets even weirder," he continued. "I decided to take a little look at Interpol's case files."

Roisin raised an eyebrow – that definitely didn't sound legal!

"And there was a file on a Sinter. It was a big file as well, several terabytes of information. But the file was heavily protected. The most sophisticated tracking cookie I've ever seen. If I'd tried to crack it, they'd have found us in a nanosecond. I've scrambled the direct route into your ISP, but there's only so much you can do against tech like that. Specially working with this rubbish equipment." He gestured with distaste at Roisin's computer. She decided to let that little insult slide.

"I figured it was best not to try it. I have no idea what Sinter is into, but it's serious stuff. And some very high-level people are looking for her."

Roisin offered to give Minh some money for all the work he'd done, but he seemed genuinely upset by the offer. He also didn't seem willing to give up just yet; the challenge had him thoroughly intrigued.

A week after Sinter went missing, Roisin started seeing faces in the shadows herself. She remembered what Sinter had said about young men, cropped haircuts, hooded jumpers too hot for the weather. All of a sudden they were everywhere. When she approached to confront them, they melted into the scenery. But when she came home to find Wolf sitting at her kitchen table, he made no attempt to hide.

She had been taken prisoner, but it had been a strange kind of capture. They had not harmed her, had not tied her up or restrained her. Indeed they had encouraged her to continue as normal, going to the centre, treating the usual patients. It was clear they were laying a trap, and didn't want her to change her life in case that alerted their target. It was almost comical. She was being ordered around by these boys who were half her age, and felt as if she should just scold them, ask where their parents were, to tell them off and send them to bed without their tea. Something about their demeanour told her that wasn't an option. There was never any sign of an adult's hand behind their movements; they were perfectly capable of making and implementing their own plans. Roisin pretended that she was playing along with their little game in order to find out where Sinter was, but that wasn't true. Actually there was something that felt so dangerous about them, their confidence, organisation and certainty . . . they really frightened her.

The Clan ruled her every waking moment for over a week. Every time she strayed from her normal path and made to head to the police or embassies, she would walk straight into a dark-eyed young man, who would shake his head, and lead her back to the centre. They never mentioned what they would do if she tried to argue – they didn't have to. She knew better than anyone that the easiest place on earth to disappear without anyone noticing is a big city. Roisin decided to play along but to keep her eyes open and her wits about her.

Finally, one evening there was a knock on the door and she opened it to find Saker staring at her. Roisin knew who he was. Sinter had spoken of a boy once or twice, of a friend that she shared a bond with, who had taught her to catch trout with her bare hands, and to construct a long bow from matured ash or yew. Sinter had mentioned him with a kind of sadness, like an old friend who was now dead to her. Even when Saker turned up on her doorstep Roisin was still hoping this would turn out to be a childish game, and that there would be some kind of happy ending. But what happened was truly shocking. Though he looked the same as the Clan boys, the others tore into him as if he was a mortal enemy. They attacked him en masse, a pack of hyenas falling as one on a stumbling, panicking antelope. For a few minutes she thought the bloodlust would be too powerful, and they would kill him, but the boy Wolf stepped in. Just like an alpha wolf disciplines his pack members with snarls, nips and bared teeth, Wolf waded into the whimpering Clan boys, and dragged them off Saker. That was not the end of his suffering, though. Every time one of them passed Saker, they would take special delight in delivering a slap, punch or kick to the cuffed boy. Theirs were not the clumsy slaps one would expect from a schoolboy either, but the short, sharp and precise jabs of practised martial artists. The crunch of knuckles on bone made her wince, but Saker took his punishment with remarkable fortitude, refusing to show any signs of pain.

Some hours later a bus with blacked-out windows pulled up at Roisin's house, and the two of them were bundled in and driven to their new prison. They had hoods placed over their heads until they were inside so they couldn't tell where they were going. For the first few minutes Roisin could track their movements by the scent emanating from a familiar bakery, or the stench as they crossed the river, but soon she was totally disorientated. The bus stopped, and they were dragged into a building and led up some rickety wooden stairs, before the hoods were taken off. They found themselves in a disused classroom. On one wall was a blackboard, emblazoned with years of chalk writing in English and Vietnamese. The windows were blacked out with tatty slatted bamboo blinds, the only illumination was the dribble that spilled in from the street outside. Their hands were tied behind their backs with cuffs made out of plastic cable ties. Then the Clan left them alone.

"You're Saker, right?" Roisin asked, and then with real concern, "are you OK?"

The boy didn't move. He didn't even groan. He just lay there, doubled up as if he had stomach ache.

"Please, say something . . . just show me you're alive."

"I'm alive," he stated with difficulty, "though don't get over-excited. I'm not expecting that to last long."

"Well, we'll deal with that problem when it comes around," she said. "How bad is it? Where do you hurt worst?"

"I think . . . everywhere," Saker responded. Painfully, he sat up, doing his own mental status check as he did so. Pain in the chest and stomach was bearable, so probably no internal bleeding; arms and legs unbroken, everything seemed reasonably clear in his head, which was good – he probably didn't have a concussion.

"Is there anything I can do?" Roisin asked.

"Yes," he replied, "you wouldn't happen to have a choc ice, would you?"

Roisin laughed out loud, then added, "and some bolt-cutters, a rope ladder and a helicopter."

Despite himself Saker giggled, then winced. Everything really did hurt.

"So, Mister, would you mind telling me what's going on?" Roisin asked.

"That is a very long story," he said.

"Doesn't look like we're going anyplace for a while," she prompted.

"Where's Sinter?" he asked.

"I was hoping you could tell me that."

Saker sighed. It was as he'd expected. "The Clan have her. They used her as bait to capture me. They knew I'd come." He shook his head. "I can't believe I was so predictable."

"The Clan?" Roisin asked. "Is that what they're called? Are they who she's been on the run from? Who are they?"

"Much as I'd love to answer all your questions," Saker interjected, "I've kind of had a bit of a kicking. And we have to think of a way out of this, or I'm going to end up being executed in a creative and very unpleasant way."

At that, the door swung open, and the boys came back. There was something different in their attitude, something inhuman. Their breath seemed too hot, they yelped and yipped in excitement, and bared their teeth at each other, threatening to fly into rages. Something primal was happening here, and even Roisin could sense it. She was shown the way, and allowed to walk freely. Saker was dragged down the corridor. He seemed to be on the edge of consciousness, and left behind smears of blood, black against the floor in the half-light.

They were taken to what had once clearly been the assembly hall of the school. It had high ceilings, and the desks had been dragged to the edge to create a sort of amphitheatre. The two hostages were taken to the centre. The Clan formed a circle around them, faces and noses twitching in anticipation. Then they fell silent. The Prophet entered, and behind him was the boy she recognised as Wolf, and . . . Sinter! The girl was dressed in simple navy Vietnamese trousers and tunic, walked barefoot, and had no tethers or cuffs. She didn't seem to be being led against her will.

"Sinter!" Roisin called out, but the girl didn't turn, didn't show any sign of recognition, of happiness or fear. Roisin had spent her life with some of the poorest people on earth, and had seen some terrible things, but this was chilling. Now the girl stood before her. Their eyes met. Roisin instantly saw that Sinter's eyes were still alive, and seemed to be pleading.

Then the Prophet spoke.

"This is a great moment. In the long history of the Clan, we have never taken on a female initiate. Today, that will change."

The reaction in the room was electric. The boys all gasped, with a mixture of uncertainty and disbelief. Saker, who had been slumped, opened his eyes and knelt upright.

"The strength of this organisation is that we evolve. As times change so do we. The time has come to bring a whole new set of skills to our order. Guile, cunning, ruthlessness.

We welcome Tigress!" The final phrase was delivered with a flourish, as if he expected a round of applause, but the boys didn't know how to react. The Prophet continued. "For two centuries, initiates have had to prove their loyalty before becoming part of us. A trial of fortitude, where they are taken to the very limit. But special times call for special measures."

With that he unsheathed a tanto knife, the scalpel-sharp cutting edge scraping against the scabbard. He turned it in his hand, offering the handle to Sinter. Both Saker and Roisin looked on, willing her to take the weapon and plunge it into the vile man, but she didn't. With a steady hand, Sinter accepted the samurai blade and turned back to her two friends.

"The woman first," the Prophet said.

The girl stepped forwards. It was as if she was in a trance.

"No. Sinter, no, it's me!" Roisin called out to the friend imprisoned inside the zombie body before her. Saker gazed, silent, too exhausted and battered to intervene. "You don't have to do what they tell you! You're stronger than that!" Roisin was crying now, but furious through her tears.

"Do it," said the Prophet simply. "Prove that you are one of us."

Sinter stepped forward, as if her limbs were being operated by remote control. She levelled the blade at Roisin's throat. They made eye contact. Roisin saw terrible fear, and a single tear slip down her cheek.

"Sinter, I don't know what they've given you, but you can fight it. Don't let him win, Sinter – come back, wake up!" But try as Roisin might, she couldn't break the terrible spell. Sinter pressed the knife to her throat.

"And now, become the angel of death – prove yourself to your brothers." The Clan were silent, poised as if to pounce. Sinter tensed her muscles and drew back to make the brutal incision. Roisin closed her eyes. Saker sank to the ground.

"Stop!" the Prophet called. "Enough. We have seen enough." Sinter dropped to the ground, the blade clattering to the flagstones.

"Remember this moment, Tigress," he said in triumph. "I can make you do anything I want. Your two friends will be waiting. Next time I ask you to perform a task for me, you will do it, or we will return here, and we will all watch you execute the two people you care most for." Sinter pressed her face into the cold tiles and sobbed.

12

Coming to from darkness, Sinter had to face the stark memory of her actions. In her mind's eye all she could see was Saker kneeling beaten and bloodied, and Roisin's frightened green eyes, utterly betrayed. She remembered that in situations of high stress, Saker had always told her to step back from the panic of the present, and go through a complete status report.

"Chest and upper legs strapped down. Movement minimal. There's no guard present, which means they must be doing regular sweeps of the area. I probably have a window of half an hour or so before they'll pass through again."

She struggled with her whole body but the straps weren't budging. "OK, so the very fact I can struggle means the drugs have a cycle of effectiveness, and right now they're not totally in control." She looked up at the drip bag that was supplying her with the noxious fluids. The liquid was as clear as water. Below it was a valve, controlled by a plastic wheel. The drugs were slowly dripping through, then down the clear pipe into the needle in her hand.

"I need to stop the flow somehow."

She struggled with her left hand, twisting it side to side, pulling backwards at the strop that held her wrist down.

"There's give there!" She clenched her fingers, as if reaching inside a narrow jar to get the last biscuit. It would come out. The only thing that would get in the way would be the needle on the back of her hand.

"That's really going to hurt."

Eyes clenched with the pain and effort, Sinter tugged backwards, while rolling her hand from side to side. The hand pulled through, and the needle tugged out of her flesh. Fluid dripped from the needle onto the floor. There was no time for elation, Sinter needed to think quickly. She was under no illusions. It would be too difficult to unbuckle the straps that held her down. There was no way to get free, but she *could* stop the drugs that were controlling her mind.

With her free hand, Sinter reached up to the white wheel and turned the valve on full. The clear fluid flowed onto the floor. "They'll notice that," she told herself. Sinter grabbed the tube and plunged the needle into her mattress.

"The needle will be getting blunt; it's going to hurt putting it back in."

That would have to wait. It was just essential to get that awful toxin anywhere but in her veins. As the mattress began to soak it up, Sinter contemplated her next move. At the usual flow rate, the drip would probably last for six hours, then someone would be back to change it. If the bag was drained too soon, then it would be replaced, and all her efforts would be for nothing. She turned the wheel off and the dripping stopped completely. Anyone who examined it closely would notice, but it was a chance she'd have to take.

Sinter had never put an IV needle into herself before. She trapped the needle against the covers, and winced as she pushed it against her skin. It didn't go in well, but enough for no one to notice unless they were looking really carefully. Minutes later, she heard the far door open, and quiet footsteps approaching. They stopped just beyond her view, but the watcher didn't speak. She could hear their breathing, sense the tension in them. Sinter longed to say something, to try and distract them, to take their gaze away from the equipment. But she had nothing to say. She lay with sweat drizzling her forehead. Surely they'd see the small patch of fluid by the bed? But then she heard the door shut. There was silence. Sinter started to count. "One one thousand, two one thousand, three one thousand." When she got to sixty she extended a finger. When every finger on both hands was extended, that made ten minutes. She started again from scratch. It was thirty minutes before the guard came again. As soon as the door had closed, she wriggled her hand free, pumped drugs into the mattress, and struggled to scratch the needle back into her hand again. By the third time of doing this, she could feel the fog beginning to lift from her mind. With the hold on her waning, she could begin to feel pain too, and also realise the true awfulness of what she had done.

It was perhaps six o'clock in the morning. After ten horrid cycles, her wrists were bruised and chafed, getting the blunt needle into her hand was like trying to push a soft crayon into a crisp apple. The IV bag was also just about empty. This time, when Sinter went through the process, she left the valve open. Her timing was perfect. The next silent guard who came in went straight to the bag and took it down.

"Thirsty!" the invisible voice commented. Sinter fought back the urge to retort, and lay staring into space, inanimate. There was a jangling sound as they began changing the bag. Halfway through she became aware of someone else coming into the room.

"Leave it," a familiar voice said. "It's time for her training."

The Prophet watched as Sinter was unbuckled and slid her feet to the floor. Sinter let her arm swing to her side, allowing the cuff of her tunic to drop and hide her bruised wrist.

"It's time," he said.

She was led down the corridor, with two burly boys standing shoulder to shoulder with her. They emerged in the assembly hall again, but now the tables had been removed, and the main space was filled with Clan members, all engaged in a martial arts class. They had paired up, and it seemed to be a free-for-all, with punches and kicks flying, and each contestant roaring with every blow they delivered, to centre their force. Though it appeared chaotic, when the Prophet entered one of the boys let out a series of sharp barking yelps, and the action stopped instantly. All the boys bowed to each other, then turned to their master, breathing heavily, sweat soaking their tunics.

He addressed them all. "It's time for you to welcome your new sister into the Clan. She has proved herself in guile, and now it's time to prove herself among you in strength." There was a derisive snort from one of the boys. The Prophet caught his eye.

"You. Death Adder. Step forward."

The black-haired boy stood a full head taller than Sinter, and was brimming with confidence. He didn't look or move like his namesake snake, but the huge dark tattoo covering his chest was just visible below the open neck of his tunic. He stood in front of Sinter, face to face. She giggled. Then looked at the Prophet. She saw he was serious and stopped smiling. Death Adder took up an offensive stance, fists raised ready to strike. Sinter stood, uncertain. Surely they didn't expect her to fight this boy? It would be a massacre!

"Begin!" called the Prophet.

She didn't even see his arm snake out at her, or even really feel the open-handed cuff to her jaw. All she knew was that she was now flat out on the floor, her ears were ringing and the Clan were baying for her blood. Then the pain hit her. Her jaw wasn't broken, but heavily bruised. Eating and talking would hurt for days. She was also horribly shaky; all the strength and aggression had evaporated from her body. Death Adder was standing over her, fists raised, daring her to get back up and take him on. That would have been suicide. Somehow she had to get the upper hand, but he was holding all the cards.

She looked up at her adversary, standing snarling over her. His namesake was the fastest-striking snake on the planet. The boy had lived up to his name. As he leaned forward, his tunic dropped slightly open, and she saw the full tattoo, an evil-looking snake with vertical slit-shaped pupils. Despite the cheering and jeering around them, Death Adder wasn't playing to the crowd, not dropping his guard to showboat or gloat over his victim. There was no suggestion of any weakness.

"Weapons!" Sinter shouted. Death Adder turned to look at the Prophet, uncertain of what to do. The Prophet also seemed caught off-guard. He lifted one eyebrow inquisitively.

She got to her feet. "Your boys might enjoy playing," Sinter said with scorn, "but it's time they grew up."

There was audible reaction to that. The Clan were incensed, growling at her defiance. The Prophet nodded, and clapped his hands. Two boys ran off, and returned with wooden staves, as long as Sinter was tall. Death Adder took his in his hand and spun it easily, expertly. A staff was thrown to Sinter and she snatched at it, fluffing the catch. It bounced painfully off her finger and clattered to the ground. The Clan laughed as one at her ineptitude. Shaking her hand and bruised thumb, Sinter knelt to pick up the stave. She threw it from hand to hand, feeling the weight of it. It looked like a broomstick, but was much heavier, made of stouter wood. A blow from this could crack her skull, end it all in a second.

"What the hell are you doing, Sinter?" she cursed herself through gritted teeth. And then it came to her. The protocol. Even when their training seemed most anarchic, there were rules. Sinter took up a neutral stance, and levelled her staff in front of her horizontally. Sensing that Sinter was showing respect, and wanting to start the bout in ritual style, Death Adder mirrored her stance, and he too held his staff out horizontally, so that the tip touched hers. They faced each other down like two swordsmen, ready to duel. Sinter bowed, and Death Adder followed suit. For a millisecond his eyes left hers. Sinter raked her stave down the length of his, smashing it into his knuckles. Death Adder yelled in pain and dropped his staff. She would not give him a chance to strike again. In a second, Sinter leapt forward, yelling in unfettered fury, and drove her weapon into his chest then, as he buckled backwards, she swung it like a baseball bat, clattering it into the back of his head. He dropped like a sack of cement.

The room fell totally silent. Death Adder lay motionless, a glossy pool of blood spreading across the floor. Sinter gasped, panting, the anger seeping from her. But then something occurred to her. She stepped forward, raising the stick above her head, as if ready to finish him off. The Prophet shouted. "STOP!"

Sinter froze, as if hypnotised by his words. It was all an act, but it was an effective one. Everyone watching believed she meant to kill him. There was a universal sigh of relief from the room.

"Take our new initiate back to her . . . *quarters*," the Prophet said. Even through his words, Sinter could hear that he was smiling.

13

Blinking through blood and sweat, Saker looked up to see the red-haired lady looking down at him. She had clearly been crying – her eyes and cheeks were red, and her nose was running.

"What have they done to her?" she asked.

Saker pulled himself up. He grimaced as he felt a sharp pain in his ribs with every breath. His face felt tender; his lip and eyebrow were split. His mind was fogged.

"I don't know exactly what they use," he replied. "It used to be something called sodium pentathol, plus a whole cocktail of other nasty drugs. Some make you tell the truth, some make you angry. Others . . . well, they just turn you into a puppet, easy to manipulate. They've been around for ever, though they're obviously illegal." He sniffed. "The Clan don't tend to worry about things like that though."

"She would have killed me," Roisin sobbed.

"But she didn't," Saker reasoned matter-of-factly.

"We're still here, which means we're still alive, and we still have a chance."

"We need to get a message to the outside," Roisin said hopefully. "Let someone know we're here."

"Have you got a phone?" Saker asked.

The sigh he received in return answered his question.

"Flags? Maybe we could do some semaphore!" Saker quipped. "Or maybe if you have a torch we could do some Morse code!"

"You lot really are the skinhead Boy Scouts, aren't you?" Her response was too weary to be a joke.

After a minute's silence, Roisin spoke again. "She thought you were never coming back, you know?"

The boy's eyes fell to the floor. "Yes. I know. I guess I got so tangled up in me, I just totally forgot she was suffering too." The shame practically dripped off Saker. "This is all my fault. I took her from her perfect life, took her from her family, got her mixed up in the Clan, dragged her halfway round the world, then deserted her. And now she's here, and they have who knows what plans for her, and I can't do anything to help."

"Are you done?" Roisin asked curtly. "Are you finished with your little 'woe is me' thing? Because just a second ago you were saying we're still alive, and there's still a chance." Saker looked into Roisin's defiant face. He had an ally, with real strength. No, they were not done yet.

The door to the classroom opened, shaking them from their determined frame of mind.

"Traitor," a silhouetted form said. "You two better be reading each other your last rites. We're shipping out. The Prophet wants both of you out of here, cargo class. It's going to be a long, rough ride," the voice laughed, and slammed the door shut behind him.

"We've not got much time," Saker said urgently. "Do you have any hairpins in your hair?"

"What do you think this is? The 1950s?" responded Roisin. Saker looked around the room desperately for anything that could help. There! On one of the noticeboards on the wall was a tack, a pin with a long plastic end to it. Saker stood up, ignoring the pain in his side, and lurched over to the wall. When he was at the wall, he turned his back to it, so his hands could grapple for the pin.

"Got it!"

He shuffled back to Roisin.

"OK, these handcuffs are just plastic cable ties. We'll never chew through them, and there's no way of burning them, but the mechanism for keeping them closed is really quite simple. Take this pin in your teeth, and see if you can press the sharp bit into the plastic lever that keeps it shut."

Roisin sat up, and manoeuvred herself into position. She bit down on the plastic of the tack, and using her tongue, moved it in her mouth until it was in the perfect place.

"You're going to have to drop down to my height," she instructed him. Saker knelt in front of her, and lifted his bound wrists to her. Roisin could see where he meant; one end of the plastic looped through a square hole, almost like a belt buckle. If she could press down the plastic locking lever, the cuffs should ease open. But how was she going to do that without the use of her hands?

Painstakingly, she leaned forward, and teased away with the end of the pin. Almost instantly she dropped it, and had to fall face-first onto the floor to pick it up in her lips again.

"This'd be a great game for breaking the ice at parties," she joked. Saker actually snorted with laughter. Anyone who could still make light of a situation like this must be a riot in normal life. Roisin had it back in her teeth again, and was fiddling with the mechanism. It was near impossible.

"Keep schtill," she mumbled. Saker willed his arms to go further back, to give her the tiniest of advantages. Yes! She pressed it down fractionally. Saker tried to pull his wrists apart, and the plastic slid a notch or two, but he had moved too fast, and Roisin lost control of the pin. It bounced off the floor again.

"Would ya stop fidgeting? That was nearly it, you big eejit."

This time, the pin slid into the mechanism, and Saker eased his wrists apart, gently, fluidly. The cuffs dropped off. With his hands free, it took seconds to release Roisin.

"What now?" she asked.

"Now we need a plan." Saker looked around, and chose a desk near to him. He flipped it onto its side, and stood on one of the prone legs. Then, he wrenched upwards on the desk, ripping the leg free. It made a pretty decent club. The two of them stood, stretching muscles that had been bound in place for too long, and Saker took up position by the door, the chair leg raised above his head.

They didn't have to wait long. It was the same silhouetted figure that came back for them. As soon as he opened the door and walked into the room, Saker brought the desk leg down with a dull *thunk*, leaving the guard unconscious on the floor. Saker quickly went through his clothing, and came up with gold dust.

"How's that?" he said triumphant, holding up a phone. "Now you'd better call the cavalry!"

Roisin took the gadget in her hand and flipped it open. She knew exactly whom she should call.

The guards had not left Sinter's bedside since escorting her back. This time she had not been hooked up to the drugs, and the strops had not been applied. The Prophet knew that he had her under control. She could sense how uneasy they were with her. They were scared. Two highly trained killers, scared of her! It wasn't entirely surprising though – she might be the first girl they had ever met. They had no idea how to talk to her, no idea what she was capable of.

But what could her next move be? Her friends were somewhere in the building, possibly being harmed. Any escape attempt would have to include them. What she needed was some kind of diversion. Lying on her back, looking up at the ceiling, Sinter felt herself slipping into sleep. As she began to dream, she saw herself and her two friends, fleeing through fields of long flowing grass, almost flying, but pursued by a pack of baying dogs. When she saw the dogs' faces, they started to morph into the forms of the Clan: one had the slit eyes of Death Adder, filled with hatred and vengeance. Another much larger than the others, had the bull-like neck of Bison. They bore down on the fleeing trio, teeth snapping shut centimetres from their heels. Then the skies above abruptly darkened, black storm clouds rampaged, lightning ravaged the heavens, and a downpour hammered onto them. She was shaken from her reverie. The clouds had opened, pouring rain onto her face. But this wasn't part of the dream – it was real! Sinter spluttered and woke, soaking wet. Water was thundering out of the ceiling. It was the fire control system. Someone had set it off. All the electrics shorted, the ceiling fans wound to a halt, the lights went out and it was almost totally black.

From the streets beyond came the sound of screeching tyres, over-revving engines and sirens. At almost the same instant, piercing white beams cut through the windows, from high-powered searchlights outside. A warped voice on a loudhailer speaking staccato Vietnamese commands resounded around the dorm. Her two guards ran to the windows to find out what was happening. What they saw outside made them gasp with horror.

"It's the army!" The first boy was Deathstalker, named after the most venomous species of scorpion on earth. His tattoo curled down his neck from his ear. What he saw was five or six cars with flashing lights, pulled up in defensive formation. Behind them, untold numbers of uniformed men with machine guns surrounded their side of the building.

"No! It's the police!" shouted Mako, the other boy, over the roar of the pounding water. "What are they doing here?" They heard more Vietnamese orders shouted out through the loudhailer.

"But we own the police!" Deathstalker yelled back. "This is ridiculous."

"Let's get her out of here," Mako replied.

"Damn right. I'm not waiting around to find what they want!" Deathstalker turned to the bed where Sinter had been sleeping. It was empty.

"No way!" The chill in their veins hit both of them, as their eyes met. They sprinted to the door, wrenched it open and ran. In the corridor beyond it was chaos. The fire system was drowning the building, Clan boys were running about in panic, desperately trying to shut it off, and come together to work out what on earth was going on. The door slammed shut behind them.

The second they were gone Sinter crawled from under her bed, where she'd been hiding.

14

The corridor was empty now, though jets of water were still hissing above. Sirens and the loudhailer echoed outside. Sinter saw her opportunity, and dashed out. She ran as far as the next corner, and looked around. Seeing two boys in an intense argument, she pulled back. They hadn't seen her. She peered around again cautiously. Their quarrel concluded, they sprinted off. Sinter followed them. She was drenched, hair plastered to her face, her cotton pyjamas clinging to her skin. Approaching a T-junction, a boy dashed across ahead of her. She ducked in close to the wall, using a meagre pillar as cover. He hadn't spotted her. But there was something about him that seemed so familiar . . .

Before she could stop herself she called out, "Polecat!"

The boy turned. It was the same face. The same slight, weaselly form. He grinned at her as if sharing a private joke then turned again and ran. It really was Polecat;

he was alive! The execution had all been an illusion, smoke and mirrors, one of the Prophet's many tricks. It was too much to take in. Perhaps it had been achieved with movie-style make-up and prosthetics, perhaps she'd simply been hallucinating. It didn't matter, she hadn't killed anyone – she didn't have blood on her hands. The Prophet's hold on her had never been as complete as he'd made her believe. Relief swept through her in waves. She wasn't a murderer. She wasn't an assassin. She had just been the victim of a conjurer's cheap trick.

And then she heard thumping boots and ducked back into cover again. Polecat was being pursued by three Vietnamese soldiers, all carrying automatic rifles. As soon as they passed, Sinter dashed out the way they'd come, splashing down the concrete floor in her bare feet. She rounded a corner and stopped dead. A powerful figure stood in a broad martial arts stance over two black-uniformed Vietnamese, who lay in the puddles. As she watched, the man despatched another policeman with a blow to the temple. The white-haired, blue-eyed monster of her nightmares looked up. She was frozen to the spot.

"Sinter!" The Prophet was soaked, his robes plastered to his sinuous form. His face was bloodied; he had clearly not had everything his way in the fight.

His eyes locked on to her, hypnotic, transfixing.

"Come to me!" he demanded. Sinter screwed up her face to tell him to go to hell, but found with horror that her body would not obey. She took a step towards him. Some of the drugs were still in her system.

"Are you responsible for this?" He gestured to everything around them: the police, the streaming water. She shook her head, a helpless child denying she'd been stealing apples from the neighbour's orchard.

"They will soon realise their mistake. Come to me." The voice had her in its thrall. Another step, then another. She was almost within his grasp. Her mind focused on tiny details, and time seemed to slow almost to a halt. A tremor rippled across one of the puddles. The sound of clattering boots resounded down the corridor.

"NOW!" he yelled. The urgency in his voice shook her out of her trance. Turning to run, she came face to face with five armed Vietnamese riot police, faces covered with helmets and goggles. They levelled their rifles at her, torchlights cutting like light sabres through the spray. She held her hands aloft in surrender, but then realised they were aiming past her, at the Prophet. All she had to do was stand aside, and he would be taken! At that second, a vice-like hand clamped over her mouth, another about her throat, and she was borne backwards, her feet barely scraping the floor. She tried to shriek, but couldn't. The police shouted orders in their own language, barking at the Prophet to let her go. Sinter could feel the fog settling over her mind again. Suddenly the chaos and noise was fading away. She couldn't hear any of it, couldn't see the ceaseless downpour, the torches or the guns. Instead, she focused on a fly, vibrating its wings on the pipes above. A trickle of water ran like a tear down the riot visor of one of the policemen. Above, on the ceiling, a gecko licked its own eyeball, she fancied she heard the slurp as its tongue lashed back into its mouth. Each individual droplet of water splashed into the puddles in slow motion, perfectly round, then exploding like diamonds and fireworks.

"Sinter!" A different voice this time. "Sinter!" She flicked her eyes to the side. "Tigress, it's me!" It was so familiar. And then another female voice.

"Sinter, Sinter honey, don't let him win." She wrenched herself sideways. Down a side corridor, just five or six metres away, were her two friends. Saker stooped, hand clasping his ribs, and was being aided by Roisin. Their hands were untied, they had no Clan guards – they were free. Her heart leapt, then her heightened senses focused on a new sound. It should have been drowned out by the screaming, the sirens, the rushing water, but to Sinter the rasping noise of the tanto knife being drawn from its sheath was nails-down-blackboard deafening. The Prophet raised the blade to her throat, and she was powerless to resist. A crack, a muzzle flash – one of the police had fired. She saw the bullet streak towards them, slowed a thousandfold in her altered perception. It grazed the fabric at the shoulder of her tunic, she felt it thump into her captor, then the grip on her throat was released.

"Run! Now!" Saker screamed. For a second she was powerless, staring down at the rifle barrels, rooted to the spot. Then she took flight.

Once more the Prophet's voice rang out, "You can't run from me!"

He was down on one knee, hand clamped over the flesh wound in his shoulder, blood running freely with the water that poured off him. His blue eyes caught hers.

"This . . . is . . . NOT . . . OVER!"

For a second she saw something that would haunt her nightmares. A predatory beast, wounded, teeth bared, ears flattened against its head. At its most dangerous. The Prophet made to stand, but was shouted down by the armed men, who advanced, rifles bristling. Saker and Roisin took her by the hand and dragged her away.

They sprinted out of the building with their hands held high in the universal symbol of surrender, towards a blinding array of lights and blaring sirens. Police ran from the mêlée, offering blankets, leading them away from the scene. There were dozens of armed men speaking into radios, sprinting around with automatic weapons, hiding behind the cars as if expecting someone inside the building to start firing on them. They were taken under armed guard beyond the first cordon to the back of a truck, where a military doctor examined their wounds. All around it felt like a war zone. More shots rang out inside. They could hear Clan boys being dragged out, protesting, fighting back against their captors.

Roisin took Sinter in her arms, and gave her the biggest hug she'd ever had. "Honey, what have they done to you? Don't worry, we'll get that vile stuff out of your system; it's going to be OK."

"It's fine, Roisin – I managed to get rid of most of it. I can feel it fading. I'm . . . I'm so sorry." Sinter's eyes brimmed with tears. She turned to look at Saker. His eyes were downcast. He looked battered.

"You have nothing to be sorry about," Roisin comforted. "It wasn't you in there . . . it wasn't you."

Sinter nodded to her friend. "So what happened? How did you get the cavalry to turn up?"

"It was Minh. Our friendly computer wiz," Roisin responded. "I called him from a phone inside. I'm guessing he called the police, then somehow accessed the school building's central fire alarm system. I don't know what he told them – maybe he said there'd been an armed kidnapping, maybe some terrorist thing. From the look of things, he told them Interpol's most wanted was holed up in there. I don't know," she mused, "you can say what you like about the kid – he may be a bit weird, and you wouldn't invite him to a dinner party, but he's a total genius."

Saker didn't want to break up the reunion, but had no choice. "We have a lot to talk about, Sinter, but now is not the time." He looked around. "Any minute now, somebody up high is going to talk to somebody else up high, the police are going to realise all of this is a big scam, and then everything will swing the Clan's way and we'll be the wanted ones again. We have to put as many miles between us and them as possible."

Roisin nodded. "You need to listen to your bird boy. Run. Run," She paused, and her voice cracked slightly, "don't ever come back."

"But what about the centre?" Sinter cried. "What about the kids, and the patients . . . what about you?"

"I never thought this would last," Roisin answered. "It was obvious there was something dark going on with you. I just didn't realise quite how dark."

"So you're staying?" Saker asked Roisin.

"There are people here who need me," responded her friend. "And I've spent a lot of time making a life here. I'm not leaving. And the Clan aren't coming after me, not when they realise you two are history."

Saker nodded. "They won't be popping their heads up in this part of the world for a while . . . not after this mess." He placed a hand on Roisin's shoulder. "Thank you for everything."

"You take good care of her," she replied.

"Forget that," Sinter was indignant. "I'll be taking good care of him." She hugged her friend one last time. Roisin nodded. Then with one last wink at them, she ran back towards the building shouting hysterically at the top of her voice.

"Help! Help! I left my handbag in there!" she yelled. The armed guards leapt up to restrain her. "You don't understand – it was a vintage Louis Vuitton!" The confused policemen swarmed around the crazed foreigner, holding her back. As she fought against their grip, Roisin risked a glance back towards the truck. Saker and Sinter were already gone.

15

Fleeing the scene was surprisingly easy. The instinct of the police and military waiting at the first cordon was to get the two civilians as far away from trouble as possible. Saker and Sinter were ushered away from the building, and out into what proved to be an abandoned industrial estate, disused and decrepit buildings, creepy and deserted in the pre-dawn night. Saker was struggling with his injuries but they ran as much as they could. They slowed to a walk whenever they saw police, so as not to attract attention. Finally they came into a district where the streetlights were working and the first people were beginning their day's work. As soon as a *tuktuk* drove by, they flagged it down, and told him to drive straight to the bar where Sinter had taught English when she'd arrived in the city. There, nestled behind a bottle of cobra whisky, were her passport and emergency cash, still there after all these months.

"Someone was thinking ahead," Saker commented, not wanting to say outright how impressed he was with her planning.

"Just think of all the drunks who've spent their last dollar in this bar, not knowing all this cash was right here," she said, hiding a smile of pride.

"And your mother's locket too," Saker noticed.

Sinter turned it over in her hand, and popped it open. The angelic face of her mother gazed impassively back, slightly faded with time. There was no mistaking the family resemblance. It was the only memory she still had of home, and particularly of her mother, who had died when she was still young. "I wonder what she'd make of all this," she said. "I'm pretty sure this wasn't a part of her plan for me."

"She'd see that her daughter is saving people's lives, thinking for herself, surviving . . . I reckon she'd be really proud," Saker said, suddenly serious.

Sinter immediately had the urge to turn on him, to demand, "What do you know about my mother?" but fought it back. After all, it was probably the nicest thing he had ever said to her. Instead she asked, "Well, a nice normal family life is out of the question now. How am I supposed to help people if I always have to be on the run?"

"I have an idea," Saker said. "A way that we can have family, and that we can do some real good. But to do that you have to trust me. And you need to come back to Borneo with me."

"Why not?" Sinter replied. "I've got nothing better to do."

Saker didn't detect the sarcasm in her tone and continued, "There are people and animals there that need our help." And then, looking at the floor, "I know I'm no expert, but I reckon some friends can be as good as family."

Sinter was genuinely touched and took his hand. "Maybe better," she said. Perhaps he wasn't so unbearable after all.

Finding the emergency stash was just the start. Saker had no ID whatsoever, nothing more than the bloodstained clothes he stood up in. They walked out of the bar with their heads down and faces covered, and flagged down a passing truck. It turned out the driver was heading west, driving towards the border with Cambodia. As the pair didn't yet have a plan, this seemed as good an escape route as any. Sinter reasoned that it was one of the least carefully watched roads out of the country; perhaps they'd be able to sneak through unnoticed.

It took a couple of hours for them to leave the sprawl of Ho Chi Minh, before the buildings gave way to the dead flat countryside of the Mekong delta. The tarmac was in places covered in rice fresh off the plants; the locals pour it onto the road to dry it out, allowing passing cars to drive over it, which separates the grains from the husks.

Dopey-looking water buffalo munched grasses and wallowed in the mud, attended to by flocks of white egrets that stabbed at the insects kicked up by the larger animals' feet. Workers in the fields plucked rice plants from the drying paddies, their heads protected from the burning sun by conical coolie hats. Some sang as they worked, oblivious to the drama passing by in the form of the two young runaways. It was about two in the afternoon, the hottest part of the day, when the truck driver warned them the border post was nearby. They asked him to pull up a kilometre short, and paid him a few dollars to "forget" he had ever given a lift to such an unusual couple. They approached cautiously down the rutted road, flanked on both sides by open fields, until they saw ahead of them the guard post that marked the border. On either side of the road stood corrugated iron shacks, with an indeterminate number of guards, smoking cigarettes, obviously bored. Even at this distance, it was clear they were carrying AK-47 rifles.

"We need to get off the road," Sinter said.

Saker looked up in surprise. "I was just about to suggest the same thing!"

They sprinted a couple of hundred metres through the paddy fields to a small wooded copse, and took up a position where they could look at what they were faced with.

"It's so flat," Saker said, nodding at the fields around them.

"Yeah, no cover at all. They'd see us trying to sneak across straightaway," Sinter agreed. "What about at night time?"

Saker bit his lower lip. "Well, they've got those searchlights, which would make it tricky."

Sinter sighed. "Landmines would be harder to spot as well."

"Landmines?" Saker asked, shocked.

"See those big sandpits?" She motioned towards features in the fields that looked like the sand bunkers on a golf course. "They're bomb craters. The Americans dropped thousands of tonnes of bombs here in the Vietnam War."

"But that ended back in the 1970s!" Saker exclaimed. The Clan had studied the Vietnam War, as any student of warfare must. The invading American forces had every technological advantage over the guerrilla soldiers of Vietnam, the Viet Cong. The Americans had modern fighter jets, helicopter gunships, and unleashed bombing campaigns of unparalleled ferocity, while the Viet Cong were fighting with ancient Russian and Chinese rifles. The Prophet had told them that the Viet Cong succeeded because they were battling to protect their land, homes and families, so would sacrifice everything, would never give up. The Americans on the other hand never really even knew what they were fighting for. They were beaten, and driven out of the country humiliated, but not before one of the most brutal campaigns in modern times. Despite the war having been over for decades, its effects still lived on.

"There was so much explosive, they've never been able to clear it all," Sinter explained. "There were also tens of thousands of landmines laid here. You should see how many amputees we get in the centre. They go to work in the fields, tread on something, and get their legs or feet completely blown off." She thought back to some of the horrors she'd seen at the centre. "Even kids . . . it's awful. Walking through here at night without torches would be crazy. Over the border in Cambodia is apparently even worse."

Saker shuddered. He would certainly be really careful about where he put his feet. They skimmed the edge of the tiny wood, looking out onto the fields and trying to come up with a strategy. Without warning, Saker's foot disappeared into the ground. Both of them yelped with horror, the unexpected motion making them react as if he had stepped on a landmine. But it wasn't that. Saker's foot had pressed through the crust of the soil, and into a tunnel below. Saker sat breathing heavily, utterly relieved.

"Don't do that to me!" Sinter hissed. "I thought you'd stepped on something! What is it, anyway?"

"I don't know," said Saker. "Maybe a rabbit warren?" He pulled the grass apart, and looked into the hole.

"That would be one big rabbit," Sinter mused.

They were looking into a substantial tunnel. It was perhaps a metre high and wide.

"Drainage pipe?" Saker asked, but as he looked around him, he already knew that couldn't be right.

"No . . . no, I've heard about these," Sinter said, excited. At the centre one of her older patients had chatted while she treated him. At the time she had only been politely half-listening, but she remembered enough. "In the war, the Viet Cong dug tunnels, thousands of them. Their soldiers would live in them for months, underground, hidden away from the American soldiers."

Saker looked at her in horror. "They lived . . . down there?"

"I know, it sounds insane!" Sinter replied. "But they had everything there, bedrooms, meeting rooms, kitchens. The Viet Cong could travel about underground invisibly; their snipers could pop up anywhere, then disappear. There are even stories about them tunnelling right underneath the American high command, and listening to the generals making their plans. They learned all of their strategy, always knew where they were going to strike next. The Americans could never figure out why the Vietnamese were one step ahead . . . but it was the tunnels! The ground here must be like Swiss cheese."

Saker looked up and towards the border. "And I'm guessing one easy way for the Viet Cong to get out of danger would be to tunnel across into Cambodia and escape to safety?"

"Well, yes!" Sinter looked at Saker in hope – maybe they could do the same thing! Then her face fell. "There's only one thing though . . ."

Saker looked at her questioningly.

"The tunnels . . . they were booby-trapped."

Saker could feel the sweat break out on his forehead. It was bad enough that they were thinking about getting into a tiny dark tunnel, which would in all likelihood have collapsed years ago, or that might collapse on their heads.

"Booby-trapped how?" he asked.

"Well, in all sorts of ways." Sinter's voice was troubled. "What I was told is that the Americans figured out about the underground cities, so had come up with ways of destroying them. They'd light fires and smoke them out, or flush them with poison gas. Then they started sending attack dogs down into the tunnels. The Viet Cong reacted by setting up mines, explosives, pitfall traps full of poisoned spikes . . . the dog handlers were so heartbroken at what happened to their dogs that they refused to let them go inside. They sent down their smallest soldiers instead. They called them tunnel rats."

Saker felt totally sick. They could go back to the city and face the authorities and maybe the Clan. Or they could try and cross the border at night and get blown up. Or they could go down into the tunnels and risk being speared or having the world cave in on them. None of these seemed like good options.

"I want to go for the night crossing – we do have one torch." Saker's claustrophobia was building so that he felt physically ill.

"Which we wouldn't be able to use above ground, cos they'd see us," Sinter countered. "It has to be the tunnel."

The boy looked down into the darkness. "I guess whoever takes the lead gets the torch?"

"Yup," said Sinter. "They also get to be the one who comes across the booby-traps first."

For most people, a tough choice. But not for Saker. There was no way he was going down into the darkness without a torch. "The tunnels it is, then." He stamped the ground till it smashed away a space large enough for him to squeeze through. There was no going back now. He took a deep breath, clenched the small penlight torch in his teeth, and slipped into the tunnel.

The tube smelled musty and damp. Roots grew through the walls, which didn't have any struts or supports, but were made of hard-packed earth.

"If they've kept the roof up for forty years, there's no reason it should cave in now," he reasoned to himself. He began to scramble forward on his hands and knees, heartbeat thundering away so powerfully it must surely be echoing along the tunnel. Behind him, Sinter dropped into the darkness, and followed closely behind him. Having her tight on his heels made him feel even more claustrophobic, but he couldn't exactly tell her to back off and feel her way around in the blackness!

After about ten metres, they came to a small cave-in. It blocked half the passageway, and they dug through it with ease, but it was a creepy reminder of how fragile the tunnels were. At least the last time he had been through this in Borneo it had been in a cavern of solid stone.

Suddenly the air exploded with the swoop of unseen objects, screeching, a rush of wind past his head. Saker screamed.

"What is it?" Sinter yelled from behind. "Saker, SAKER, it's just bats!"

Taking his hands from his face in shame, he realised it was true. Black-bearded tomb bats – this must be their day roost and they'd been disturbed by his movements.

"What the hell is wrong with you?" she chastised him. "We're on a stealth mission, and you're supposed to be a trained assassin! When did you turn into such a nervous wreck?"

"I just had a bad experience . . . in a tight spot. It freaked me out a bit. But I'm OK."

"D'you want me to go first?"

"NO!" Saker replied too quickly. "No. I'm fine. Let's just get this over with."

As they crawled on, his torchlight illuminated scorpions and whip spiders scampering off at the first sign of light. Ahead of them a snake beat a hasty retreat. Saker wasn't too worried about that. This part of the world had some of the most venomous snakes on earth: cobras, kraits, the king cobra, Russell's viper, but they were the least of his worries. Snakes have no external ears, but can hear by dropping their jaw to the ground, transmitting vibrations to the inner ear. He knew they would be able to sense the vibrations of his movements, and would disappear, not wanting to risk a confrontation.

The tunnel opened into a chamber about the size of a small caravan, not quite big enough to stand up in. Three bunks had been carved into one wall – the soldiers had spent their nights here. Rotting old blankets lay on the beds, the floor was littered with discarded, yellowing magazines. In the centre was a rusty metal stove attached to a gas canister. Above their heads a pipe led to the surface, doubtless to make sure fumes from the stove didn't build up inside the room. There was a table, dusted with earth that had fallen from the roof. On top was a US army helmet and some rusty bullets. They found a bayonet-style dagger, and put it into the backpack. Around the walls cubbyholes contained bottles of whisky, books and tinned foods. Inside one was the sinister smiling face of a child's doll, its decayed threadbare blonde hair and milky blue eyes made it into a horror film character. It seemed so out of place. Sinter reached to pick it up. Saker saw her movement out of the corner of his eye, turned, and shouted. "NO!"

She stopped dead, the doll in her hand, just millimetres above the cubbyhole.

"Do not . . . move . . . a muscle," he instructed her.

Walking over, he cautiously peered behind the doll. A thin wire led from it to a round metal object tied to the wall. It was a grenade, and the wire was tied to the firing pin.

"Put it down, very, very slowly."

Sinter did as she was told, her forehead beading with

153

sweat. She could sense the terror in his voice. When it was down, she stepped backwards. They both breathed out with relief.

"The perfect booby-trap," Saker explained. "Soldiers know better than to pick up anything that looks like explosives, so they booby-trap unusual things, objects that make people curious."

"But a doll?" asked Sinter.

"Is perfect – it doesn't fit in, and seems so harmless. And it was the one thing you picked up, so it very nearly worked."

"That's it," she said. "I'm not touching anything from here on in. I'm following you!"

The tunnel led on in the direction of the border. They had to drop onto hands and knees, scrabbling in the dirt, trying to ignore the creepy-crawlies and the overwhelming sensation that the world could cave in at any second. Saker had the feeling that something had changed. All of a sudden the sense of enclosure had increased. What was it? He stopped, and sniffed the air. Nothing – it was just as musty as before. Then he tried the trick of lifting his hand up, trying to use the hairs on the back like whiskers to sense the movement of the wind. Again nothing. That was it. There was no wind moving through the passageway any more.

"I think there's a blockage up ahead," he whispered.

"Well, let's carry on, see what we find."

Another few minutes of shuffling, and they found

the reason for the airlessness. But it wasn't what they'd expected. The tunnel came to an end, but not in an untidy roof collapse. Instead it was a neat vertical wall, and at the base of it was a hole, filled to the brim with water.

"What the . . . ?" Saker puzzled.

"Flooding?" Sinter mused.

"I don't think so. It looks deliberate to me."

They both surveyed the obstacle, trying to figure out what it was.

"You know what you said about the Americans trying to flush out the tunnels?" Saker asked.

"Yes . . ."

"You said they smoked them out?"

"And used poison gas as well." Sinter suddenly saw where he was going.

"The gas or smoke would travel right through the tunnels . . ."

Sinter finished his sentence. "But if there was an area that was filled with water . . ."

". . . a swimthrough, or sump . . ."

"Then that would stop the flow of gas or smoke."

Saker tried to imagine what it must have been like. The horror of fighting trapped here, with savage dogs coming after you. Pistols firing in an enclosed environment would have been deafening. Screams as poison gas filled the chambers, having to hold your breath and duck through the black water to get to safety. It must have been terrifying.

"The bit that's filled with water wouldn't have to be very long to stop gas moving through," Saker reasoned.

"Only a metre or so," Sinter agreed, trying to sound upbeat.

"So we're going to have to swim it."

Now Sinter felt sick as well. The idea of dunking in the dark water, not knowing what was beyond, horrified her. But they had no choice. Saker knew he had to be brave. He lowered himself into the murky water. It was surprisingly cold. He started breathing deeply to fill his lungs. Then took Sinter by the hands.

"If I don't come back . . . I'm sorry for everything."

"What? Don't talk crazy, Saker; this isn't the time for it." She tried to sound cross, but couldn't keep the fear from her voice.

"OK. Well, if I don't come back, then go back to Ho Chi Minh. Go and turn yourself in to the authorities, tell them you want to speak to Interpol, tell them everything."

She looked him in the eyes, and nodded.

Saker took four deep breaths, clenched the torch in his teeth, and ducked underwater. And then Sinter was alone, and in total darkness.

She fought the urge to panic, to scream, and finally closed her eyes. It seemed to take an eternity, but then Saker burst up through the water, gasping for breath.

"It's only a short duck, maybe two metres!"

Sinter could put it off no longer. She took a last few deep breaths, which were almost like sobs. Then she dropped into the murk. The second she was immersed the breath seemed to vanish from her lungs, and she had to fight not to suck in water. The flooded tunnel was no more than the width of the hole in the middle of a car tyre – squeezing through it while underwater chilled her soul. If the tunnel had narrowed, there would be no way to back out. She would drown there. Thrashing in blind terror, the need to breathe was overwhelming, but then strong hands took her wrists and pulled her forwards. She gasped, surfacing alongside Saker and instinctively hugged him, shaking with cold and fear.

"That was so horrid," she sobbed.

Saker couldn't think of anything to say that would make it better. Truth was that her warmth and presence actually made him feel more comfortable too. Knowing that he was helping Sinter took his mind off his own terrors. He held her until the sobbing eased, then clambered out, wiping the water from his face.

They were in another tunnel now, and began the long crawl anew. Within minutes they were both sweating again. She could hear Saker counting ahead of her.

"What are you doing?" she hissed.

"Counting metres. I reckon we've done five hundred. About five football fields. We don't want to pop up short of the border – or on it! We're probably over halfway now."

Abruptly he stopped, and Sinter crawled over his heels. "What is it?"

"Come see," he said. She squeezed in alongside him.

His hands had collapsed a shallow pitfall trap. The top had been covered over with brittle sticks and sand. Inside the pit were wicked spikes. He had narrowly avoided impaling himself.

"Doubtless they'll be smeared with something nasty," he said matter-of-factly. "We were taught to make pitfalls not to kill, but to maim. They just give you a nasty wound, then bacteria and grime get in, and make you sick. It's harder for an army to treat someone who's badly injured than a dead body."

"That's cold," Sinter said, disgusted.

"That's war," Saker agreed.

They clambered over the top of the spikes, and carried on. Was it Saker's imagination, or was the tunnel getting narrower? They were no longer on hands and knees, but on bellies, scrabbling forward on their elbows. This was awful. He could have lain there and wept.

But then there was a light. A laser-thin shaft of sunlight.

"Sinter! There's a hole in the roof up ahead!"

"Are we far enough on? Will we be over the border?"

"I don't know!"

The urge to scrabble and burst into the fresh air was fierce, but he must not. He approached quietly, and put his head up through the hole. He dropped straight back down inside.

"What did you see?"

Saker hissed at her to be quiet. Then after a minute he whispered back. "We're right on the border. It's about three metres away. There's a barbed wire fence, and a guard with a rifle walking along it. Give it five, then we carry on."

Now at least they had their bearings. They needed to cover another few hundred metres before they would be safe. They were both almost frantic, the sense of doom overpowering. Suddenly a column of dust fell from the ceiling into the torchlight. He stopped dead. Then another slightly bigger fall. He looked up in dread. Then the ceiling collapsed, burying him completely.

The air was filled with dust, a tiny sliver of light cut down from the surface.

"Saker!" Sinter screamed, scrabbling in the dirt to try and dig her friend out. He had been buried alive.

16

Fingernails tore into the mud, scraping away the heavy blanket of earth that covered Saker.

"Come on, come on," Sinter urged, hoping any second he would come to and battle his way out. But he did not. She uncovered a leg, entombed in the soil. She followed it to his chest, and hauled his body out. There was no sign of breathing. She shook him, shouting his name, trying to get some response. Then her medical training kicked in. Flipping him over to face the floor, Sinter drove the heel of her hand between his shoulder blades, emptying dirt out of his mouth. Turning him back, she put her finger into his mouth, cleaning out the mud, and making sure he hadn't swallowed his tongue. Once more she turned him and slapped his back. He choked, showering dirt from his throat, before collapsing into a coughing fit. He was alive!

She used the tiny beam of light from the torch to

illuminate his eyes. They were wide with terror. She had to get him out of there, and fast.

"Follow me!" she ordered. They scrabbled through the last few hundred metres scraping their elbows and knees, and finally saw sunlight ahead. Sinter popped her head up. They were surrounded by trees. Relief drenched her – she could have sung with the sense of freedom. The undergrowth obscured any view, so she slipped up through the hole, and crept to the edge of the woods. Pulling the ferns aside, she peered back towards the border. It was plenty far enough away. Returning to the hole, she dragged Saker up into the dappled light. He seemed totally spent.

They sat there and looked at each other.

"We made it," Sinter said.

"Yup. I have never been so happy to see sunshine," Saker said.

"So what now?"

Saker shrugged. "Find something to eat? Somewhere to sleep? Then we push on for the capital."

"Phnom Penh?" she asked. He nodded.

"I need some ID. And we need a plan."

Saker breathed in the moist, growing smell of the trees. It smelled like life. The ground beneath his feet was soft, like a thick shagpile carpet. Had it really been less than a month since he had been in the forest? This was a closeness that didn't make him feel claustrophobic . . . he was home!

They pushed on for a kilometre or so, until they came to a stream, flowing clear, babbling over mossy stones. Great vines hung over it, and exotic birdcalls resounded around the open glade. It was perfect. They dipped into the water, washing off the grime that had ground into their skin and impacted under their fingernails. Wasting no time, they guzzled down the life-giving water, scrubbing the bugs from their scalps. After a long mouthful of water, Saker looked up at his friend. This was not so far from how they had first met. He had surprised her at a waterhole as she came down to bathe. Back then he had thought her an annoyance, a troublesome, pampered little girl. That little girl had just saved his life, and he hadn't even thanked her. With wet black hair plastered to her face and shoulders she seemed to be taller than he remembered, and there was a presence about her that radiated confidence. Suddenly he was shy. Perhaps it was those amber eyes, piercing even under the grime.

Grabbing a handful of damp moss, he moved towards her. "You've missed a bit," he said gruffly, self-conscious. He wiped away some of the smear from her cheek with the moss, using it as a sponge. Sinter was surprised. Such affection was not like him. "Thank you," he said simply.

"For what?" she replied, slightly caught off guard.

"For saving my life."

She snorted, but he wouldn't be fobbed off.

"I've always thought I could do anything, that nothing scared me . . . but I was terrified down there. Useless. If you hadn't been there, I'd have been buried alive," he shuddered.

"And if you hadn't been there, I'd have been blown up by a doll! So we're even."

Saker shook his head. "I've never been so frightened."

She looked at him keenly, with new interest. "Something's happened to you."

"It's a long story." His eyes studied the leaf-litter. "But before I came to find you, back in Borneo, I was trapped underground. I thought I was going to die. Long and slow. The darkness isn't my friend any more. And caves and tunnels . . ." he shuddered again.

"We have a lot to catch up on," Sinter said, reaching for his hand. He looked down at her fingers, but she merely took the moss sponge off him, and started scrubbing at her cheeks, gleeful at the thought of getting clean.

The streamside was perfect for a camp. They set to finding food, fire and shelter. Propping sticks against the side of a big rock made the framework of a lean-to. Next they found a massive rainforest tree that had collapsed, leaving a hollow trunk on the ground. There was no point in sheltering inside it – too many biting bugs and mites called chiggers that buried beneath the skin would be living inside. Instead, they stripped great chunks of dry bark from the fallen forest giant, and stacked them against the stick frame, making a simple tent. Sinter made a carpet of sweet-smelling ferns.

Meanwhile, Saker gathered firewood for fuel, and fungus that could be ground down to make tinder, the smallest and most flammable ingredient in fire-making. He stripped the bark from a stick of hardwood, then tore a chunk of softer araucaria wood, and placed that onto a flat banana leaf. Holding the stick between his palms, he pressed the point down into the soft wood and began to roll his hands together, drilling it into the softer base wood. After several minutes the stick began to bore a hole, then a thin plume of smoke started to grow. After fifteen minutes, the sweat was pouring off his forehead, and his shoulders and forearms were searing with the effort. Finally a nugget of compacted fine wood dust dropped onto the banana leaf. Saker blew on it gently. It glowed bright, with the tiny ember within it. He added kindling, then larger wood, until half an hour later he had a fire burning. Sinter sat close, to dry her clothes, and stave off mosquitoes.

So with water, shelter and fire, they could address the grumbling in their stomachs. They split up to try and gather some food. Saker's search ended with a palm tree, about ten metres tall.

"Jackpot!"

The leaves were shaped like the back end of a trout: a fishtail palm. The fruit he knew to avoid, as it contained a nasty stinging chemical, but the flowers were extremely useful. He gathered armfuls of them. Around the core of dead sections of the palm was woody material that would make exceptional tinder for lighting future fires. Next to the mature palm tree was a smaller fishtail palm. He pushed it down, then peeled off the bark, to collect chunks of the starchy yellowy core: palm hearts, one of the most nutritious and delicious of all bush foods.

Next he searched around for giant bamboo. He found a stand of the mighty grass, with trunks as thick as his upper leg. Using the bayonet he hacked one down. The interior was hollow, but contained natural dividers. Saker chopped them up into pots.

Sinter came back with malva nuts, Chinese chestnuts, and fruit from sacred lotus. These pink flowering plants float on the surface of ponds. Each one has a fruit that's almost like a seed-dispenser, and has about twenty hard seeds inside.

"The villagers used to grind these into flour back home," she told Saker, "but they're kind of fine just cooked a bit." They placed them onto a flat rock on the edge of the fire, and waited till they blackened, then crunched them down. Two green bamboo pots were filled with water, and placed close to the embers. The young leaves of the lotus went into one brew, the flowers from the fishtail palm into the other.

Half an hour later, they were tucking in to a remarkable feast.

"These are amazing," Sinter announced, crunching up sweet palm hearts.

"I'm not quite so keen on the lotus seeds," said Saker. "They're really bitter. It kind of tastes like when you suck on a biro and the ink leaks into your mouth!" Then pointing to one of the bamboo pots, "Mind you, those palm flowers should sweeten them up a bit."

Sinter reached for the darkening green pot, and yelped as she singed her fingers. Using some of the moss to protect her fingers from burning again, she lifted it to her lips. A look of surprise at the first sip.

"It's like honey!"

"It can be used like syrup – it's great stuff!" Saker said. "Don't drink all of it; that's dessert!"

By now the forest was hidden by night. Outside the living room created by the firelight, the orchestra of the evening was tuning up. Frogs belched, twanged and peeped, crickets chirruped, and there was monotonous droning from cicadas in the treetops. Saker felt utterly at home for the first time in weeks. He watched intrigued as a bright green praying mantis, as long as a pencil, walked up one of the logs as if to wander right into the fire. It stopped just short of the flames, swaying side to side, its triangular head and massive eyes twitching. Then Saker saw what it was after. A moth fluttered closer, attracted by the light. The mantis snapped out, snatching the moth with ferociously barbed forearms, then drawing it in. The decorated wings were snipped off and dropped into the embers below, where they sprang into flame like old parchment.

"So what do we do now?" Sinter finally said.

Saker stared into the hypnotic fire. "Get some sleep, I guess."

"No. I didn't mean right now. I meant what are we going to do? With the future."

"Ah," Saker replied. That was a much bigger question. "I was wondering when we'd get to that." He nibbled his lower lip. "I guess I've been putting off thinking about that."

Sinter sighed. "The last six months have been the best of my life. Working with Roisin, helping people."

She told him everything. About the ramshackle centre, treating elderly patients with festering wounds, or children with malaria. She told him how it felt to save a life. How it felt to see the gratitude in the eyes of a mother whose child you've made better.

"It's made me feel . . . worth something, like I can make a difference."

Saker nodded, but didn't look up at her even once. He just gazed into the fire.

"I don't want to be on the run for ever. I want to help people," and then, her head dropping, "but I guess that's impossible now."

Saker shook his head. "I don't think so."

All of a sudden, he was transported back to the very last time he'd sat round a fire like this, with the faces of his Penan friends dancing with fire sprites. He thought of Hagen, the bespectacled figure, whose quiet controlling hand had done so much to help their cause.

"At the centre, did you ever break the law?" he asked.

"No!" she replied. "Everything was legal. We worked like crazy, but it was always above board."

"And so you helped one person at a time? Perhaps ten people in a day?" he asked. "It's all pretty small-scale, isn't it?"

Sinter bridled with anger. "What's that supposed to mean? Are you saying that we should just ignore people who are suffering? What have you ever done to help anyone?"

"Nothing," he replied. "I've never done anything really worthwhile. And I don't mean to be rude about what you've achieved. I think it's wonderful what you've done."

He stopped, struggling over the words. "But it strikes me that there are an awful lot of bad people prepared to break the rules, and they're the ones who succeed, while all the good people sit around with nothing, battling the system. It's the corrupt officials who end up running the world, the drug dealers who get the power, the criminals who are the millionaires. That's exactly why the Clan is so powerful: because they operate outside of the law. I'm beginning to think that if we really want to make a difference, maybe we need to be prepared to . . . well, to do the same."

Sinter was about to react angrily, but suddenly remembered the shipment of out-of-date medicines Roisin had taken from the Irish hospital. If they'd obeyed the rules, those drugs would have been thrown away, and hundreds of people would have gone without treatment. They *had* needed to bend the rules to get what they wanted. She hesitated. "So what are you suggesting?"

"When I left you in the Himalayas, I needed to go back to the forest. It's where I feel at home. It took me a month to get to Borneo – it's one of the biggest islands in the world. Loads of jungle, mountains . . . it's paradise. Or it was, not so long ago. I wandered on my own for months, but finally I found them."

"Them?"

"The Penan," he explained. With that he reached inside his tunic and pulled out the carved crocodile amulet, hanging on its leather string. "They gave me this to show they'd accepted me."

He told her about the Penan. About how they were battling to maintain their ancient lifestyle in the face of the modern world. He told her about Lars Hagen, and what he'd tried to achieve. And then the story of the cave. The paintings of the Penan, and the orang utan, timeless faces without friends, at the mercy of progress. Finally he got on to the uprisings against the loggers, and told her about the sabotage.

"The Penan are a Clan. The right sort of Clan. Good people. But they have nothing, so they have no power. If they obey the rules, they will die out, disappear. The rich people who want their lands will take everything until there is nothing left. The only chance they have is to go outside the law. They're failing, and they're fading away, but that's only because they have so few tools. And because they know nothing of the modern world."

They sat in silence, thinking.

"So what are we going to do?" asked Sinter. "There's just the two of us; how are we going to change things?"

"There's not just two of us," Saker replied. "We have the Penan. We have Hagen. Strikes me that's enough for our own Clan. And now we have Roisin, and even more importantly we have your friend Minh."

"Minh!" Sinter retorted. "How's he going to help? Nothing's going to make him leave Vietnam!"

"This is the twenty-first century," Saker responded. "He doesn't need to leave Roisin's kitchen, as long as he's hooked up to a computer. Anybody who's got a brain like his and doesn't mind breaking the rules can bring down a big company with a couple of taps on a keyboard."

Of course! Sinter hadn't stopped to think of the great potential of Minh's devious abilities. In the city, he'd managed to foil the Clan with no more than a few minutes' hacking. The internet could span the globe in a millisecond.

"And I'll bet you anything that someone like Minh has hacker friends all over the world who are just as capable as he is."

"You don't know Minh," Sinter laughed. "He doesn't do friends." She had never met a less sociable person in all her days.

"Well then, we need to convince him to *make* some friends," Saker countered. "Roisin could do that, surely?"

Sinter nodded. Yes, that would work. "But what for? I mean, what is it you're hoping to achieve?"

Saker looked up from the flames, and met her eyes. "You and me. We're starting a new Clan. And we're going to change the world."

17

The rain came down that evening as if trying to batter its way into their fragile shelter. The two of them had started by lying as far from each other as possible, but then as the rain sucked the warmth from the night, they crept closer and closer together, until eventually Sinter felt an arm reaching around her and drawing her in. At first she tensed at the unfamiliar contact, but the body heat was so welcome that she soon relaxed, and they dozed together, the cut-grass smell of the ferns soothing them to sleep.

When she woke, she instantly noticed the lack of Saker's arm, but heard the crackle of the smoking fire, and knew he would already be at work finding their breakfast. They did make a pretty good team! Sitting at the fireside yawning and rubbing her eyes, which stung from the smoke, she was in for a surprise. Saker turned up grinning from ear to ear, his shirt lifted into an apron and full of fruit.

"Mangoes!" said Sinter, delighted.

"Yup, and they're good and ripe!"

Saker had also found a handful of seeds and leaves, which he held out excitedly.

"What are those?" Sinter asked.

Saker picked out from the embers one of the bamboo containers, which was filled with hot water.

"Try rubbing some of them in your hands with the water," he instructed.

Sinter reacted with glee as lather sprang up between her fingers. "Bubbles!"

"Yup, these are from a soapnut tree. It's incredible stuff – anti-fungal, anti-bacterial, beats any nasty chemical soap."

Sinter was just about to go crazy, and have her first proper bath in weeks, when her expression turned serious.

"Well, the first thing we need to do is give your wounds a good going over. Last thing we need is infections."

Saker looked down at himself. His knees and elbows were grazed and torn from crawling through the tunnels, but he could feel his face and head had worse wounds where his Clan brothers had beaten him. Using moss sponges and the soapberries, the pair of them cleaned out each other's wounds, making sure no grit was left inside. They grimaced and winced, but knew it was essential.

Early morning in the forest was a delightful time. The humidity washed away by the previous night's rains, the constant drip, drip of water off leaves punctuated by the songs of fairy bluebirds, babblers, spiderhunters and sunbirds. The glorious fluted burble of an oriole singing nearby, the crash through the canopy above as unseen monkeys swung through the treetops. It was blissful. Finally, having gorged themselves on sweet mangoes, the pair covered the fire, hiding all traces of their camp. The beams from the rising sun were like arrows, directing them to the west. They walked in single file, Sinter taking the lead, following what looked like a game trail. The undergrowth had been worn down in a line no more than a hand's breadth wide; vegetation to either side was bowed away from the track. In the mud were the cloven hoof prints of sika and muntjac deer, and occasional pad marks of a leopard cat, crisp and clear. It had been stalking the trail as they slept.

Both were immersed in the big ideas of the previous night's conversation, lost in the soundtrack of the morning, until there was a sudden "click" from under Sinter's foot. She stopped dead. That wasn't a twig breaking.

"What is it?" asked Saker.

"I don't know," she replied, standing stock-still. "I've trodden on something."

"It's just a stick," Saker said, willing it to be true. "It must be a dry twig." But as he said it, he looked around at the sodden world. It had been raining all night long. There were no dry twigs here.

"Stand still," he said, his voice catching in the back of his throat. Dropping to his belly, he wriggled forward, and ran his hand over Sinter's foot, and into the leaf-litter below. She stood motionless with fear. His fingertips brushed aside the leaves. Under the sole of her foot was a dark green metal object, the shape of a flying saucer and the size of a dinner plate. In places the paint had peeled off, and revealed red brown rust.

"What it is?" she asked.

Saker closed his eyes. "It's a landmine."

Sinter fought back a sob. "Why hasn't it gone off?"

"It's a pressure mine. Most go off straight away, but some are armed when you tread on them. They detonate when you step off again."

"What am I going to do? I can't just stay standing here!"

"It's pretty old," he mused. "Must have been here decades. It probably won't work."

Sinter shook her head. Countless people had come into the centre missing their feet or legs. These landmines would continue claiming lives and limbs for generations yet.

"I wouldn't count on that," she said, with a bravery she didn't feel.

"No," he replied matter-of-factly. "No, we can't count on that."

His mind was racing. They'd come so far. He couldn't lose his Clan so soon! Without saying another word, he dashed off into the forest.

"Saker?" she called. Then again, more desperately, "Saker! Where have you gone?" She willed herself not to move a single muscle. All of a sudden it felt as if her whole body was starting to sway – the urge to run, or jump, was enormous.

Meanwhile, Saker was busy. He cut a long wooden stave, and gathered some fibrous palm leaves to use as a primitive rope. He dropped these off on the trail behind Sinter.

"What are you doing?" she asked, struggling to look over her shoulder at him.

"Don't move!" he ordered, before running off into the trees again. This time he dragged back a huge deadfall log, probably as heavy as he was. Next, using the palm leaves, he bound the bayonet onto the end of the stave, so it formed a lethal-looking spear.

Going down on his belly again, slithering closer to her feet, he spoke. "OK, this is going to be awkward. So no sudden movements."

"Saker," she ventured.

"Please, I'm concentrating."

She shook her head. If the mine went off she might lose her leg, but his face was just centimetres away from it.

"Saker, you have to leave me. You know you do."

"That's not going to happen, so save your breath."

"It's my own stupid fault. I was in the lead; I knew the risks."

Saker ignored her, and eased the blade of the knife in under the sole of her shoe.

"If I jump for it, I'll probably be fine," she said.

"Do you mind?" Saker berated her. "Just let me get on with this. And stop wobbling!"

He could feel the metal of the detonator now. There was a pressure plate about the size of a two-penny piece with a firing pin beneath it. Millimetre by millimetre he slipped the blade between the plate and the sole of her shoe.

"If this goes wrong . . ." She was fighting back tears. "Please, I don't blame you for any of this. Actually, you saved me."

Saker didn't reply; sweat was running into his eyes but he couldn't wipe it away.

"If you hadn't taken me, I'd have been a slave. A forced marriage to an evil man . . . my life would have been terrible. This last year I've seen the world; I've found my purpose. I've had a hundred lifetimes. It's been incredible. We've had a great adventure. I should be thanking you."

Despite himself he snorted with laughter. That was a good one. The bayonet was now completely between the firing pin and the underside of her foot. Moving more slowly than he ever had before, Saker eased backwards, keeping the bayonet in place by putting pressure on the stave it was attached to. He then rolled the deadfall log until it pressed down on the stave.

"What are you doing?" she asked.

"Well, if this works, the weight of the log will keep the knife pressed down on the firing plate. When you step off, it should keep it held down, keep the pressure on, and it shouldn't . . . it shouldn't fire."

"And if it doesn't work?" She already knew the answer to that question.

"It'll work," he said.

"If it doesn't work, I'll never have to buy a pair of shoes again," she tried to joke. He didn't laugh. "I can't do it," she said.

"What do you mean, you can't do it?"

"I mean I can't bloody do it!" she snapped. "I've been standing here without moving for an hour. My legs have gone to sleep."

"It's OK," he said. "I'll help you." He walked round to face her, and took both her hands in his.

"NO!" she protested. "If it goes off . . . you need to be miles away!"

"One," he counted.

"No! I'm not going to do it!"

"Two."

"Three."

He pulled her towards him, she stepped off. Instantly her legs crumpled with the effort, but he held her upright. They stood there for a second.

"It worked!" she exclaimed.

Then they turned around. The deadfall log was slowly shifting backwards.

"Run!" Saker shouted. He dragged her along, her legs like jelly, then the whole world seemed to explode. There was an enormous boom! The air filled with dirt and twigs. For a second he was deaf, a ringing noise filling his head. Rolling on to his back, he looked at his feet. They were still there. Then he saw her beside him.

"Sinter, Sinter!" A quick look confirmed that she hadn't lost any limbs. He grabbed her and rolled her over. She opened her eyes and smiled.

"Like I said. A big adventure. Huge." She coughed a leaf out of the back of her throat. "Just think, I could be missing all of this!"

The two of them dissolved into fits of giggles.

The Cambodian forest still had a few more surprises in store. Perhaps a kilometre deeper into the forest, Saker pulled aside the leaves of a leaning banana tree to reveal a giant face. The stone image towered above them, the grey of the rock stained green with moss and algae. Its rounded, smiling face gazed down on them.

"It's the Buddha," Sinter said.

"He looks pretty happy with himself," Saker added.

"Of course he does," Sinter responded. "He found enlightenment and made the world a better place!"

"Sounds pretty good," Saker mused. "Can't be that hard, surely?" They grinned at each other.

As they continued, more and more stone marvels loomed from the eternal green.

"They used to have one of the greatest civilisations here," Sinter explained. "A thousand years ago the Khmer empire was the greatest on earth."

"What happened?" he asked.

"They destroyed themselves," she replied. "There were too many people, they cut down their forests, killed all the animals, poured garbage and sewage into all their rivers. After that there were torrential floods because there were no trees or topsoil to stop the water raging. Then there was terrible drought because they'd destroyed the natural waterways. Eventually the whole thing just fell apart. People got sick from the poisoned water, everyone either died of famine or plagues, or left the big city and went back to the country."

"It's good to see we're learning our lessons!" Saker said. "That's exactly what they're doing now in Borneo. No one seems to think about what happens when you hack down a whole forest."

"It doesn't make any sense. This same thing has been happening for ever – how can people not know?"

"They do know," said Saker. "But it's like I said; the people in control are rich. They know that when everything is used up and things start going bad they can leave, set up somewhere else. It's the ordinary people who live here who have to pick up the pieces. I'll bet you anything that the Khmer kings and queens didn't die of starvation when all this fell apart."

The statues, buildings and stonework had been consumed by the jungle. Another few hundred years and it would have disappeared behind the green.

"This must have been a thriving city," Sinter said in wonder.

"Yup, but I reckon no one's been here for years," Saker said.

"The whole country is full of temples," Sinter replied. "Some of them have just been taken by the forests."

As they walked on, they saw endless signs of the once-mighty city. Framed by dripping leaves and vines, huge friezes carved out of stone showed ancient battles, kings riding chariots, aiming their spears at their enemies. Beautiful women in elaborate headdresses danced across the tableaus, and dragons and eagles soared overhead. The tangled roots of banyan trees and strangler figs forced their way through the buildings, seeking out moisture between the stones, and over the ages forcing their way inside. Given time, a spindly root could shatter stone, or uproot a building of hundreds of tonnes. They walked in silence, filled with awe at the ruins, imagining them alive with monks and soldiers. Bright green lizards stood motionless on the stone, bathing in pools of sunlight.

Even with the landmarks of the mighty overgrown Buddhas, the forest was endlessly confusing.

"How on earth are you supposed to navigate through all this?" Sinter moaned. "It all looks the same."

"It's a nightmare," Saker responded. "The jungle is always the worst place to find your way through. We need to get to high ground."

They trudged on, in what they hoped was the same direction they'd been heading since daybreak. Eventually, the land to their right abruptly steepened, and they both started to climb. At the top of the hill was a crumbling stone temple. Saker made to climb up it, using a Buddha statue as a handhold.

"Don't!" Sinter stopped him.

"Why not?"

"I don't know," she admitted. "That's someone's God. Someone spent months making it, then prayed to it, put their dreams there . . . it seems disrespectful."

Saker was about to retort that no one had seen it for centuries, but actually felt that she had a point. He climbed by a different route.

The top of the temple broke free of the forest canopy, and gave them a view that stretched to the horizon. Beyond the reaches of the jungle, rivers and rice paddies glowed golden in the sunlight. To the far west, they could see the sky was more yellowy grey than elsewhere, the taint of human pollution.

"Phnom Penh. The big city," Sinter said.

Saker sighed. "Much as I'd rather stay here, that's where we need to be."

18

With just a few days in the forest, their ears had become used to the orchestra of the birds, frogs and bugs, so now the whine of mopeds and blare of truck horns seemed angry, violent, intrusive. Saker visibly winced at every passing vehicle. As Sinter had become a city girl in Ho Chi Minh, she found herself taking the lead, ordering a *tuktuk* to take them to the seediest part of the city. What they needed would hardly be available on display in just any shop. Shanty villages on rickety stilts teetered over black, oily streams; mothers slept on street corners with their babies clasped to their tummies. This was a part of Phnom Penh that foreigners never visited. People stared at them as if they were aliens.

They approached everyone they passed, saying, "We need to buy documents."

The response was mostly blank uncomprehending faces.

"Passport?" they then tried, holding up Sinter's own passport to try and get the point across. Finally, a boy of maybe ten years old took Sinter by the hand, leading them deep into the slum. It was a risk to follow, but they had little choice. He took them to a street given over to a Chinese laundry, neon signs in Mandarin script hanging vertically down the walls. Hundreds of white sheets were strung across the alleyways drying, and it was fiercely hot with the scorch of the driers and the washing machines. Men worked stripped to the waist or in grubby white vests, chain-smoking cigarettes.

"No, no," Sinter said, pulling back against the boy's hand, "Passport, we need to get a passport."

The boy insisted and dragged them inside, past the arguing workers. He led them to a corridor that continued downstairs to the basement. They exchanged a worried glance, before following him.

What they found at the bottom of the stairs took them by surprise. Instead of a sweaty, dirty cellar, they found an air-conditioned workshop, with modern computer equipment, several different types of scanners, and a huge printing machine. A thin man in his fifties looked up sharply as they entered, and barked in Chinese at the young boy. The boy responded just as aggressively, gesturing to Saker and Sinter.

"What do you want?" asked the thin man.

"I need papers," Saker responded. "Really good ones."

"OK," the gaunt man answered, and rifled through a

set of prints in front of him. He picked up a passport, and threw it to Saker. "One of these costs five hundred dollars."

Saker leafed through the booklet. It was an American passport. He turned it over in his hands, then turned his nose up.

"This is no good. The binding is fine, and the cover looks OK, but there's no chip in it, no Ivisa, no encrypted data on the photo. It might work for some outback border crossing, but I need something that can get me through an international airport. This is amateur stuff."

Sinter sucked in a breath. Why did he have to be so rude? They needed this man's help, and Saker had just insulted him. Sinter waited for the man to explode and throw them out of his workshop. But a smile cracked the thin man's face.

"My apologies. I don't get many connoisseurs here." He pulled another document from under the pile in front of him. "One like this is five thousand dollars. It'll get you wherever you want, as long as the airport doesn't pick you up with facial recognition software."

Saker turned it over in his hands as if it were a diamond tiara. "Now that's more like it."

It took nearly a week for the forger to make Saker's new identity. This and the trip to Borneo would use up all of their remaining cash reserves, but when Sinter questioned this, Saker replied, "It's OK – we're soon going to have more money than we could ever use."

She knew that he had a grand plan. That it involved Borneo, saving the Penan, and the orang utan, but she had no idea how they were suddenly going to get rich. When she asked what he meant, he just said, "trust me."

That really got her worried. It struck her that "trust me" is what a thief says, right before he steals your wallet. However, she was seeing a new side to Saker, a side that was more human than she had imagined possible. Whatever he was working on, it was clear he thought it was going to do some good.

They bought flights from Cambodia to Borneo, and contacted Roisin, to let her know they were alive. Roisin chatted openly with them, confident she was not being watched. After the chaos of the city, it seemed the Clan had disappeared. The raid on the old school hadn't been reported in any newspaper – it was as if it had never happened. No sinister callers had knocked at her door again, and she hoped they never would. After Sinter said a tearful goodbye to the friend who had done so much for her, Saker asked to speak to Minh. The pair of them then had a web chat that lasted all day and most of the evening, until the internet cafe owner had to throw him out onto the street so he could close the shop.

Standing at passport control, the pair had to battle to keep their fear hidden. The queue dwindled, until Sinter stood in front of a stern-looking official. Her eyes flicked from the photo and up to Sinter, and then she scanned the document. The stamp thumped down on an empty page and she passed it back to Sinter. Saker had taken a different queue, so that if one of them was caught the other could still make a break for it. The procedure was the same. The official opened the pages and leafed through it. Suddenly he stopped dead. Saker stiffened.

"You come here from Vietnam?" the man asked. Saker nodded. The man studied him.

"My family from Vietnam. Not good country like here," he passed the passport back. It was all Saker could do not to sigh with relief.

Neither of them had thought any further than getting through security. Sinter relaxed and was chatting merrily away, but as they joined the queue to get on the plane, she noticed that her companion hadn't spoken in ages.

"What's the matter?" she asked.

"It's . . . nothing," he replied.

"Don't be ridiculous – you're sweating. And you haven't said anything since we got through security."

"I don't know. Guess I hadn't thought about being trapped in a metal tube for three hours without being able to get out," Saker responded.

That was all they needed! Saker's time in tunnels and caves had created a claustrophobia worse than even he had realised. But there was no backing out now.

As the plane taxied to take off, Saker looked so frightened that the stewardess came to ask if he was all right. Sinter was really scared that he was going to tear off his seatbelt and start trying to get out. Once they were airborne though, he calmed down, and eventually fell fast asleep, leaving Sinter to look out the window at the sea passing far below them, and think about what might lie ahead.

When the sea gave way to land, Sinter was taken aback. She'd expected to see Borneo covered with jungle, but instead all she saw were ploughed fields, barren land, plantations stretching off to the horizon. How were they going to help orang utans if there was nowhere left for them to live? Was this just a lost cause?

"Don't worry," Saker reassured her, "it's not all like this. Yet."

Once they landed in Kuching, they transferred to an even smaller plane, which took them to an airstrip that was little more than a grassy field. Around it were scattered a few tin-roof shacks with wire mesh fronts, selling faded packets of sweets, dried fish heads and packet noodles. Sorry-looking dogs panted in the shade licking at their scabs; the dusty trails were stalked by goats and cockerels.

"Is there any rainforest here?" Sinter asked. "I thought this was supposed to be a jungle island!"

"There's still a fair bit left," Saker responded, "but it's

going to take some getting to. It'll be worth it though; I guarantee you'll agree."

They carried their bags down stilted wooden walkways to a milk-chocolate river, which wound lazily round the town.

"That's our boat," Saker said, pointing.

"You have got to be kidding me," Sinter replied. It was certainly a remarkable-looking craft, but had not been designed to travel on water. In fact, it was a World War Two bomber plane with the wings cut off. Half a century of modifications later, the outdated aircraft had been converted into a boat. Of sorts.

"I hope that's watertight," Sinter commented.

"Of course," said Saker, "they were built to be *air*tight, after all. And they very rarely sink."

Sinter did not look impressed. "I haven't come all this way to drown in some leaky . . . thing."

"Don't worry," he reassured her, "the crocs will get you long before you drown."

Even the hybrid boat-plane thing was not the final stage of the journey. It took them several hours upriver to the last reasonable-sized town. There they hired a longboat to get into the mountains and find real forest. The boat was a single tree that had been carved out into a basic dugout, with an engine at the back and a long pipe leading to a propeller. They sped through small areas of forest, not so different from those she had seen in Cambodia. Exotic hornbills flapped overhead, their beating wings making a sound like a steam train passing. A shape in a tree made Sinter grab the boatman in excitement. "Stop!" she cried.

As they got closer, they saw an orange form moving easily through the treetops. "Orang utan!" she whispered.

"It's a male," Saker said. "You can tell from those massive cheeks."

She looked up in wonder. It seemed bizarre that such a massive beast could be so at home in a spindly tree; the largest tree-living animal on earth. He peered down at them, but didn't seem overly interested, pausing only to pull some twigs laden with foliage into his mouth.

"The name means 'man of the forest', doesn't it?" Sinter asked.

"Yup. And if the forest goes, the orangs go too. They'll become ghosts of the forest."

"So this is what we're here for," she said. It was beginning to make sense. They passed through thick vegetation, lianas dropping down to the river. She half-expected to see Tarzan swinging on one, yodelling as he went! Crocodiles splashed towards the water as they passed, and the sounds of frogs, bugs and birds were loud even above the whine of the motor. When the forest abruptly gave way to plantations, all of that changed. The palm trees stood in neat lines, their boughs heavy with great clusters of fruit, like oversized bunches of plum-coloured grapes. Saker asked the boatman to slow his engine again.

"Do you hear that?" he asked.

Sinter strained to listen. "No, I don't hear anything."

"Exactly," he said.

She nodded. It was totally silent. If this was forest, the noises from all the animals living there would be deafening, but instead it was eerily quiet.

"Logging companies cut down the forest, and plant these trees. The fruit is used for palm oil. It's found in soaps, cooking oils and stuff, it's worth a fortune. Sometimes they buy the forests fair and square, but if they can't do that they just take them. The local people still live in tiny villages and have no contact with the outside world, so there's nothing to stop the big companies doing exactly what they want," Saker explained.

"And I suppose the palm oil trees grow really well on jungle soils?" Sinter asked.

"Yes and no. The soil here is actually really sandy. It's kind of useless. The forest binds it together. When you lose the forest the soils don't last long." He spread his hands in a gesture that encompassed the green plantation around them. "In a decade this will be a desert."

It all seemed impossibly bleak. How could they make a difference to something this big?

"We can't stop the production of palm oil altogether," Saker continued. "What we need to do is something to

make sure they don't just take *all* the forest. But we need
help."

The longboat chugged upriver and inland for three days,
far away from the last vestiges of civilisation. The first night
they stayed at a village with big satellite dishes. All the locals
were dressed in Western clothing. Small children with
runny noses chased mangy dogs down rickety boardwalks.
The racket of crowing cockerels and the call to prayer
from the town mosque woke them long before dawn.

Next day they got back on the river in their longboat,
and within minutes were lashed by a tropical downpour.
Sinter had never seen rain like it, even home in the
foothills of the Himalayas. The rain made patterns over
the surface of the brown waters, raindrops bouncing
frantically back towards the clouds. It seemed as if the
rain was trying to batter them into submission, they were
soaked to the skin within seconds, their teeth chattering
with the cold. It seemed impossible they could be so
freezing right on the equator! Just half an hour later the
rain stopped, the clouds abruptly cleared, and the world
started to steam. Mist hung over the surface of the water,
and the water steaming off their clothes made them look
as if they were smoking. Sinter was overjoyed to see the
sun, but just an hour later was praying for the rain again!
She had never been so hot in all her life. The humidity

was overwhelming, it was as if they were breathing the steam from a kettle. Discomfort was tempered by wonder. They were in the heart of Borneo, where the logging trucks had yet to penetrate. The jungles bustled with birds, and the people who lived there rarely encountered the outside world.

The villages at the riverside were made from bamboo and rainforest timbers, and the people were from Iban tribes. The Iban's chins, arms and shoulders were covered in deep blue tattoos – swirls, stars and animal shapes. In one village Sinter watched, fascinated, as an elder tattooed one of his tribesmen. He mixed soot with water, and dipped a sharp sliver of bamboo in the mixture. The younger man was clearly battling to hold back the tears, as his skin was punctured over and over again to make the design.

"If you can withstand the pain, you've earned the right to be a man," Saker explained. The Iban had earlobes that were cut into loops and hung down to their shoulders, and their hair was cut into strange-looking shapes, as if someone had just planted a pudding bowl over their heads and cut all the hair below it. At the riverside were huge longhouses, some several hundred metres long. All the families of the tribe lived together in these stretched communal homes.

Towards the end of the day, they were looking for a village where they could spend the night. Eventually they saw a stilted community coming out of the mist, but the boatman showed no signs of stopping.

"Here looks good," said Sinter.

"Here no good!" he replied, and pointed to a white flag flying over the dock. "This flag, she mean bad things happen here." He made a sign, slicing his finger across his throat. "Maybe there is someone kill here. No welcome."

The pair exchanged glances. "Bad things" covered an awful lot of ground. Maybe sickness, maybe a fully fledged blood feud. Whatever, there was no way their boatman would consider stopping.

Just as dark began to fall, they reached another small settlement. It consisted of one longhouse, perhaps fifty metres long. As they pulled up at the dock, the house emptied, and everyone in the village poured out to see them. The tattooed tribesmen made the first move – they were hostile, faces snarling, fingers toying with long machetes they call *parangs*. The women held back, their children hiding behind their legs, terrified at the strange outsiders. Luckily Saker and Sinter had come prepared, and laid out presents of tobacco, fishing lines and betel nut. Many of the local people constantly chewed on betel nut, as it gave them a mild happy feeling. They had to spit out blood-red goo every few minutes, and it stained their teeth and lips bright red.

One man in a headdress of white feathers took the lead. The way the others deferred to him suggested that he was the head man. He looked through the offerings critically, then nodded his head, and led them to the longhouse. Sinter was struggling to control her yawns, and desperately wanted to put her head down and sleep. But this was not going to happen. Their arrival was the most extraordinary thing that had happened in the village for many months, and the villagers seemed to expect a performance, as if the pair were part of a travelling circus. Inside the longhouse, they squatted around a hearth, where a roaring fire burned, and were surrounded by the entire village, who sat and stared at them. Occasionally one of the older women would wander over, and pull some of the hairs out of Saker's arms or pull Sinter's hair. The resultant yelp would make the whole village fall about in hysterics. Several of the men started to perform a story, dancing in the firelight, taking on the characters of animals in the forest as they re-enacted a famous hunt. An old woman, naked from the waist up, started playing a reedy flute, blowing into it not with her lips, but through her nose.

The rest of the women went through everything in the pair's rucksacks, oohing and aahing at every new wonder they found. The laptop and mobile phones they fingered as if some kind of witchcraft. Books and photographs were handled with awe. Pens and sweets they distributed around the group freely. One of the women grabbed a new shirt Sinter had bought in the city, and started to pull it on.

Sinter went to take it off her. "Give that back – you'll stretch it!'

"No!" Saker said, "let her take it; that's rude."

"Why?" Sinter was indignant. "We've already given them loads – they can't just take all our stuff."

"The whole idea of possessions is different out here," he told her. "Everything in the village is shared, and belongs to everyone. Some of their languages don't even have words for 'mine' or 'yours'. They don't even have a word for 'thank you', 'cos it's assumed that you'll always help someone if you can."

"That's just weird," Sinter said.

"Well, not really. I guess you could argue that owning stuff doesn't make people happy. You can never have enough, you always want more, someone always has more than you . . ." he was warming to his theme. "People work their whole lives to get stuff, then die and leave it behind! On the other hand, if my stuff is also your stuff, then no one can get jealous, no one steals, no one feels hard done by. And if you need something, your neighbour gives it to you, knowing eventually you'll give them something back, and it'll all even itself out."

"You sound like the Prophet," said Sinter.

Saker flinched, but then nodded. "Actually it is exactly how we lived in the Clan, and it's the one bit I still believe in. We don't *need* any of the stuff we're sold in the modern world. Who needs a hundred choices of breakfast cereal? People here work a few hours a day to get the food they need, then spend the rest of the day playing, relaxing, talking, living their lives. It's easy to say, but it's a much happier life than people live in cities. Everyone here is just one big family."

"Unless they're eating each other," said Sinter, pointing up into the rafters.

Hanging underneath the beams was a line of human skulls. They were clearly very old, dark brown, and with paste in the eye sockets filled with gemstones. Each had a ring of small red feathers round the crown.

"That's not something you talk about," replied Saker under his breath.

A small child who'd been watching Sinter from across the room crawled over into her lap, curled up and fell asleep.

"It's as if they've never seen outsiders before!" Sinter said, still trying to disguise her yawns.

"Maybe they haven't," Saker said. And then addressing the boatman, "What do you think? Do outsiders come here much?"

The boatman seemed thoroughly uncomfortable, and hadn't said a single word all night. "I don't know – these people are barbarians." And then, crossing himself, he added, "I not sleep tonight."

"Well, you're welcome to stay awake. I reckon Sinter and I will sleep like babies, won't we?" The question was directed to his friend, but as he looked over, he saw Sinter curled around the small child, and already fast asleep.

Next morning they breakfasted on boiled rice and rock salt, before taking leave of the villagers. The woman who was wearing Sinter's new top went to take it off and give it back, but Sinter motioned to show she should keep it. The lady beamed with pride, taking Sinter's two hands in hers and touching them with her forehead. A few minutes later she returned with a folded banana leaf, which she pressed into the girl's hands. It was full of boiled hen's eggs. The whole village gathered to watch them go. Nobody waved, they just watched in silence as the longboat started up and pulled away.

Two more hours upstream, and the longboat driver pulled in to a beach, and said he was not prepared to go any further. He made excuses about needing to be back in town, and about the boat's engine needing repairs, but they could tell he was afraid. The Iban had a reputation for being headhunters and cannibals, and until quite recently this was true. They had long given up their warlike ways, but their grisly history meant many feared to head into their lands. Saker and Sinter shouldered their packs and stepped ashore.

Sinter noticed the change in Saker instantly. He seemed to spark into life as soon as his feet touched the leaf-litter of the jungle floor. He took his shoes off so he could feel the dead leaves between his toes, and as they walked he reached out for scented blooms and brightly coloured beetles, like a toddler loose in Santa's grotto. At night they constructed shelters from a sheet of plastic he'd found on a city rubbish heap and brought with them. They cooked noodles and rice, spiced up with a few local greens. For protein, Saker dug around in a rotten tree trunk, and pulled out huge wriggling grubs. They were like oversized maggots, the size of his thumb, but with imposing black heads with scissor-like jaws. Sinter recoiled as Saker took the head between thumb and forefinger, bit off the rest of the body, munching it down raw.

"Nooooo! That's disgusting!"

"Have you tried one?" he challenged.

"There is no way I'm eating a caterpillar – that's sick!"

"They're not caterpillars, they're beetle larvae. They live in the rotten wood for years before they turn into adults . . . they're good!"

Sinter was not one to shy away from a dare, so took the larvae as he had done and, with her eyes tight closed, bit into it.

Her eyes opened wide with surprise. "It's like . . . like warm scrambled egg!"

Saker grinned. "I told you they were good!"

"Can you find any more?" she asked.

Next morning, Sinter was woken by an astounding sound. It started as a distant whoop, whoop, whoop, which built to a frantic crescendo like some kind of alien ray gun. "It must be gibbons singing," she thought to herself.

Standing up, she walked barefoot to the fire, moving quietly so as not to wake Saker. She stirred the embers, there was life in them and smoke drifted skywards. Yawning, she rubbed the sleep from her eyes, then stopped dead. She was being watched. There was movement in the bushes just beyond the clearing. A pair of human eyes focused on her. And then she became aware of another pair of eyes, and another. A bow drawn with its arrow focused on her, a poised spear held in uplifted hand, faces covered with warpaint. The hidden warriors had silently surrounded them; they were totally at their mercy.

"Saker," she whispered. "SAKER. Wake up!"

The boy roused himself, grumbling. "What is it?"

"We're in big trouble."

19

The frowning faces glowered from the shadows. A long blowpipe was levelled at Sinter's chest, doubtless containing a poison dart that would bring a slow, painful death. There was a sinister scraping sound as a machete was drawn from its sheath. Sinter didn't know much about headhunters, but the name itself was enough to strike a chill in her heart. Saker had talked much of the Penan, and how they had never indulged in cannibalism, but had said nothing of the other tribes of the region. All she knew were the few horror stories the boatman had told them. He had said that many Iban peoples had a warlike tradition. For hundreds of years villages would have raided their neighbours, kidnapping their children and eating the adults. The idea was that by eating the flesh of a powerful adversary, a cannibal could take on some of their powers and abilities. Blood feuds ran for generations, territories were fiercely protected, and because of this outsiders were not welcomed. She backed away slowly, lifting her hands in the universal gesture of surrender, showing her hands were open and not concealing any weapons. A firm grip took her upper arm.

"Don't move," came Saker's calm voice in her ear.

"That's easy for you to say," she stammered.

"They're checking us out. Figuring out if we're a threat." He stepped forward, his palms upwards, open and outstretched.

"And what if they think we are?" she whispered. "Do the Iban still eat people?"

One particularly frightening-looking man stood up slowly. His muscular physique was emphasised by stark tattoos, dotted lines along his collarbones, whirlpools on his chest.

"I'm not sure these are Iban," Saker said. Ever so slowly he reached into his tunic, and pulled out the amulet that he wore around his neck. The carved wooden crocodile. He yanked, breaking the leather thong that secured it, and tossed it to the man in front of him. Then Saker pursed his lips, and started to imitate the "whoop whoop whoop" song of the gibbons.

"That's amazing!" Sinter said.

"Let's hope they think so."

The muscular man stepped forward and plucked the amulet from the ground.

"Lars Hagen," Saker stated simply. "*Orang putih di utan.*" *The white man of the jungle.*

The man turned the carving in his fingers.

"You think these are Penan?" Sinter whispered.

"They're not the family I know," he responded. "But they look like Penan to me."

"And Penan don't eat people?" she queried. "They're peaceful, right?"

"Well . . . let's not organise a celebratory barbeque just yet."

The muscular man seemed to have made up his mind. He turned and walked off. His compatriots did the same.

"So what now?" questioned Sinter.

"I think we follow them," replied Saker, grabbing his pack.

The tribesmen moved deceptively quickly, like clouded leopards stepping lightly down almost invisible game trails. They never stopped to drink or to rest, and Sinter found herself having to jog to keep up with them. She'd not had time to put her shoes on, and was not yet adept at spotting thorns, and was constantly stubbing her toes on fallen branches. There were ten men in the group, none taller than Sinter, their wrists encircled with rattan and rope bangles, but otherwise wearing only dark hide loincloths. One had a live piglet in a string bag over his shoulder, another had sheaths of a kind of flat leaf under one arm, presumably for roofing material. Sinter decided that they were on a foraging trip, and not out with sinister intentions.

As the daylight began to fade, one of the paths widened, and they broke into a clearing. To one side, the canopy opened to reveal a panorama of emerald-encrusted mountains and lowland forests below, and to the other side, clearly built to make the most of the view, was a wooden house. There was a broad balcony at the front, a thatched roof held up by stout hardwood pillars. On the steps leading to the building sat a European man, wearing round glasses, whittling a piece of wood in his hands.

"Hagen!" exclaimed Saker.

"Ah," the man responded, in a manner that suggested this did not altogether fill him with delight, "you're back."

"I found the way out of the cave," Saker eagerly said.

"So it would seem."

"And I have a plan," Saker continued, "an idea. But we're going to need your help."

20

The security guard stopped – he had heard something – and swung his torch around at the dustbins. What was that noise? Here in a Bornean city it could be anything, from a scavenging macaque to a lost palm civet or ground squirrel. All was quiet again, and the guard relaxed and went back to walking his beat. Down among the rubbish bins, Saker and Sinter breathed a sigh of relief. They were focusing on one special office building, which was located in the middle of a dazzling modern marina. By day it was full of tourists and businessmen, but for security reasons the whole area was off limits by night. It had become a dark, silent ghost town, the kind you'd expect to see stalked by zombies in a B-movie.

Sinter felt a sense of déjà vu about the whole scene, it was not the first time that Saker had dragged her on a midnight mission dressed up in black pyjamas like a ninja!

First they'd snipped through the chain-link fence, before scrabbling along the ground on their bellies and running for cover. The building was ahead of them, thirty storeys of circular glass, illuminated by spotlights at ground level. Due to its dual functions as home of both the Malaysian environmental protection agency and the Malaysian logging industry, the building had high levels of security. They needed to be vigilant. Saker took a laptop out of his shoulder bag, and put on a headset, which had an earpiece and microphone. There was also a camera about the size of a lipstick, which he positioned over one ear. He opened the laptop, and a window popped up. The moving image from Saker's lipstick camera started playing through in real time. The horizon was a little wonky, so he adjusted the camera to put the picture straight. Now it reflected exactly what Saker was seeing. Next he activated the internet connection, and within seconds Minh came into contact. Saker could see him sitting in front of Roisin's laptop in her flat in Ho Chi Minh.

"Are you getting this, Minh?" Saker asked.

"All I can see is a shot of myself," Minh responded. "How about you actually point the camera at the building?"

Even with his pixellated image being beamed from a different country, Saker thought, he still manages to be utterly obnoxious!

Saker looked straight at the building, training the camera on their target. "Right, how's that?"

"Better. Look up," Minh said.

Saker did as he was told. "It's all vertical, polished glass," he reported. "Impossible to climb."

"Actually it was climbed in the 1990s as a publicity stunt," Minh said. "What you mean is YOU can't climb it."

Sinter stifled a snort of laughter.

Saker bit his lip and fought the urge to react. "OK, so it may be climbable," he reasoned. "But at night it's lit up, and in the day there are thousands of people here. The climb would take several hours . . . it'd be much too visible."

"Agreed," said Sinter. "Minh, could you take out those lights?"

"Of course."

"Or we could take them out the old-fashioned way?" Saker suggested.

"So either I bring this company to its knees with a few taps on my keyboard, or you throw bricks at their lights?" The scorn in Minh's voice could have stripped paint. "This is the twenty-first century."

"Yeah, and some of us step outside and have a look at the real twenty-first century every once in a while," Saker snapped.

"Play nice," Sinter urged gently. He could hear that she was on the brink of collapsing into giggles, and all his anger evaporated.

"You're right, Minh," Saker said by way of apology, "and besides, even if we took out the lights, and I climbed to the top of the tower, we'd still not be able to get into the actual building."

"I think we're going to need to be a bit more cunning about this," Sinter mused. "Minh, what can you give us from the outside?"

"Limited," he replied. "What I need is to get one of you inside, and place our own intercept transmitter on their Wi-Fi system. That way all of their communications will be going through me."

"And where's that?" asked Sinter.

"In the basement, probably," Minh answered. "When I have eyes inside, then we can move to stage two."

"Which is?" asked Saker.

"You wouldn't understand," Minh responded. It wasn't an insult; it was a statement of fact. "But I'll need one of you to get into the target's office."

The pair looked at each other. "That could be interesting," said Saker.

Sinter frowned, then looked at the dustbins they were hiding behind. "I think I might have an idea . . ."

Getting hired by the company that provided cleaners for the building was easy. Sinter was presentable and charming, and came armed with a hefty number of forged references. Figuring out how to get the intercept into the building, and how to find the main Wi-Fi router was another matter.

Everybody who entered the building had to pass through an X-ray scanner, and a metal detector. In the end, they relied on old-fashioned detective work. They based themselves in a cheap travellers' hostel, poring over plans by night, and watching the car park by day, until they spotted a pattern. One of the workers routinely came in late, around half an hour after everyone else was already inside.

Sinter studied his car numberplate through binoculars, and passed on the details to Minh, who punched some numbers into his computer back in Vietnam.

"That car's owned by Abdurrahaman Hasan," Minh told them.

Sinter was about to ask how on earth he managed that, but knew the response would only be, "You wouldn't understand."

"OK," she said, "so what now?"

"Send the equipment we need to Hasan by first post," said Minh. "It'll arrive on his desk at about nine a.m. Which means you have about thirty minutes to come through and take the package . . ."

". . . before he turns up at work and opens it," Sinter continued. "But what if he comes in on time that day?"

"Then you get caught, and go to prison," Minh replied.

"Or if someone sees me taking the parcel?"

"Then they think you're a thief, and you go to prison."

"And what if I get seen going into the basement?" she queried.

"Let's put it this way: you're going to have to work very hard not to go to prison," Minh said. Sinter's eyes widened in surprise. It sounded almost as if Minh was making a joke.

"I kind of feel like I'm playing at being James Bond," she joked.

"James Bond would never dress that badly," Minh responded. She looked down at her grubby janitor's overalls. She had to admit, he had a point.

On her first day working for the cleaning company, Sinter showed her pass and walked through the scanners. She picked up a rubbish bin, and started to walk around the ground-floor offices. Not many people were in for work yet, and most of the desks were empty. She had to work fast. There were thirty floors to the building, and hundreds of people worked here – how was she going to find Hasan's desk? Passing one of the workstations, she looked around, judged that no one was watching and picked up the phone, pressing "0".

The female voice on the end of the phone answered, "Hello, this is the operator."

"Hi, it's Val up on the fifth," Sinter said breezily, as if she and the operator were best pals. "I've had a letter dropped by for someone called Abdurrahaman Hasan, and he's not on this floor. Any ideas where I should drop it?"

The operator replied, "Just give it to the mailboy – he'll reallocate it."

Sinter paused, stumped. Then she had a brainwave. "Listen hun, actually I've seen Hasan in the canteen, and he's kind of hot. I was thinking this might be a great way of getting to talk to him," Sinter giggled self-consciously. "You know, all casual – someone sent me your mail – what are the chances?"

The operator laughed out loud. "I like your style – wish I could be that gutsy! He's on thirteen, in accounts. Good luck!"

Sinter sighed with relief. She got into the lift and pressed the button for the thirteenth floor. Just as the doors were closing, a large, imposing man pushed the doors aside and stepped inside. He was wearing an expensive suit. Even his tie must have cost 500 dollars, Sinter thought.

"Selamat Pagi, *good morning* Pak Amir," said the lady next to her, bowing her head in respect. Of all the luck! This was him: Amir, the very man they'd come to destroy! Sinter tried to merge back into the walls of the lift, making herself invisible. This gave her a bit of a chance to study the man, whom she'd come to think of as the devil himself. As she watched he excavated an ear hole with the overgrown nail of his little finger. Many of the Malaysian elite grew this fingernail long – it was a visual symbol of their status, showing they didn't have to do manual labour. She shuddered.

Saker had only shared his plan with her when he

reached the Penan. Finally he had told her that what he planned to do was to halt illegal logging and building of oil palm plantations for as long as possible. It was Lars Hagen who had suggested Amir should be their target. He told them that Amir was both the minister of the environment, and of forestry – responsible for both protecting the forests, and cutting them down! His corruption meant that he was at the centre of all of the trade, both legal and illegal, that was destroying the Penan's forests. Hagen suggested that if they could shut down Amir, then they could do something big to alter the balance of power in Borneo. The clever parts of the plan had come from the only person who really understood the powerful technological world Amir lived in. And that person was sitting behind a computer console in Ho Chi Minh.

At the thirteenth floor, Sinter apologised, and exited the lift.

"Hey!" Amir stopped her. "What is this?"

Sinter froze. "I'm sorry, Bapak?"

"There is another lift for cleaning staff," he said haughtily. "Do not ever let me see you using this one again."

Sinter kept her eyes cast down to the ground. "Of course, Bapak, my apologies." She left, dragging her bin, hearing the tuts and feeling the sneering displeasure behind her. She allowed herself a small smile. Knowing what the man was like would make what they had to do so much easier.

On floor thirteen, she had a different problem. The

mailboy had not arrived, and the desks were starting to fill up with people. Sinter found Hasan's desk, and started moving slowly around the office, emptying out waste-paper baskets, occasionally wiping her cloth over someone's computer screen. On one screen something caught her eye. It was a yellow sticky note, posted on the side of the screen. Written on it were two words:

Yayasan1989
Ferrari1989

Sinter stiffened. It was exactly the sort of thing Minh had briefed her to be on the lookout for – a login, both the username and password! She hadn't believed him when he had told her how lax office workers could be about their security, but it was obviously true. Not wanting to draw attention to herself, Sinter took a biro from the desk and scribbled the characters onto the palm of her hand. At that moment, the mailboy came into the office. Sinter tracked his progress round the room, mostly ignored by the workers as he handed them their mail.

"Come on, come on," she whispered impatiently under her breath, working her way closer to Hasan's workstation. Finally, the mailboy placed a big yellow envelope on Hasan's desk. Judging it perfectly, Sinter walked up, picked up Hasan's waste-paper basket and poured the contents into her bin, then nonchalantly swept the yellow envelope into the bin. Sweat breaking out on her forehead, she turned to leave.

"What are you doing?" a harsh voice stopped her. She turned around. A stern-looking middle-aged woman was standing just metres away from her. "Answer me!"

"Well . . ." stammered Sinter, "I thought . . . it looked like rubbish."

"Don't give me that," the woman snapped back. "Rubbish is supposed to be collected in the evenings. After we finish work, not before. We don't want cleaners round the office while we're trying to work. I will report you to your superiors!"

Sinter blinked. "No of course not, ma'am. I'm very sorry, I won't trouble you any more." And, bowing her apologies, she headed out into the hallway. In the janitor's storeroom she dumped the bin, and opened the envelope. Inside were an earpiece and a small transmitting device. She put it into her ear and switched it on.

"Minh. Minh, can you hear me?" she said.

"That is the best piece of equipment on the market," he responded through her earpiece. "You don't have to shout."

"OK, so I have the intercept. Now you need to guide me to the router," she said.

"Ride the lift down to the basement," he instructed her.

Sinter did as she was told, this time taking care to use the service lift. Once there, she walked along shelves laden with decades-worth of paper files, and into chilled concrete rooms lined with whirring computer servers, storing data from all over the world. As she walked, she described what she saw to Minh.

"Now I have loads of wires running down the walls, leading to big boxes, kind of like filing cabinets. They're light grey and warm to the touch."

"Follow the wires away from the boxes," he instructed. "At some point they'll pass through a wall-mounted box, probably glass-fronted."

Sinter followed the wires through several rooms, praying nobody would turn up and ask what she was doing. She had no answer prepared other than that she was lost.

"I think I've found it!"

"Describe it to me."

"Well, it has a glass front, two small aerials coming out of the top, and on the front of it are three bars of lights."

"All showing green?" Minh asked.

Sinter answered yes, then went on to describe the make and model of the unit.

"Right, so you need to affix the intercept to it. It should be relatively easy – just pull the wires out of the top and put them into the bottom of our unit. Then reconnect the wires to the top."

Sinter worked away, wiping sweat out of her eyes. Her heart was pounding. There would be no excuse if she got caught doing this! "OK, Minh, I think that's done," she said with relief.

"Just a second . . . yes, I've got it! So now all Wi-Fi information is running through our intercept before being transmitted out to the World Wide Web."

"Essentially we can watch what anyone in the building is saying online," Sinter ventured.

"Right," said Minh, "now all I need to do is log in to their system remotely, and get into their security. It's child's play. I just need to hack into the system."

"You don't even need to do that," said Sinter. "I think I may have a password and username for you." She relayed the characters she had taken off the computer screen on the thirteenth floor. Minh had even said "thank you"!

Sinter's last action was to hide the intercept box. Then all she had to do was return to work, and spend the rest of the day keeping a low profile, pretending to clean. It wasn't hard; for most of the workers someone of her status was as good as invisible. This gave her the opportunity to surreptitiously take photos, and make a map of the layout of the building. Amir's office was out of bounds, she would have to leave intel on that key room to Minh's ingenuity. Before she left through the scanners at the end of the day, she dropped her earpiece into a bin. Now, all that remained was to watch, and wait.

For a few days, it all went quiet for Saker and Sinter, with a sense of the calm before the storm. Minh was busy hacking into the office's systems, taking control of the closed-circuit television and watching the movements of

Amir and his secretary. Saker and Sinter set to figuring out how to get into Amir's office.

"Why can't we just get me in as a cleaner, like you?" Saker asked.

"Any time a cleaner is in his office they are watched – his secretary will be in there with them. Amir considers us the 'untouchables' – he doesn't like or trust us," Sinter answered.

Saker mused, "What about breaking in overnight?"

"You could," Sinter said, "but Amir brings his laptop in his briefcase every day, and takes it home at night. Without access to it, this is pointless."

"Can we get in through the windows? I could abseil down to one."

"They all open from the inside only; it'd be a way of getting out, but not in." Then, feeling, as if she was putting a damper on everything, Sinter added, "Sorry to be so negative!"

"How's about we make him leave the office? I don't know, set off the fire alarm or something. I could be there already, then get to work while he's out."

At that point Minh, who had just come online chipped in, "We won't need to do anything to get him to leave. Take a look at this."

With that a window popped up on their laptop, showing footage from a video surveillance camera.

"This is Amir's secretary's office – he passes through it to get to his own office. There is no camera in Amir's office.

217

Watch this carefully. 09:00 hours, Amir arrives at work. Notice he has his briefcase, and walks through to his office. 09:03 Amir comes back out, and leaves the room. 09:11, Amir returns holding coffee, and goes back into his office."

"He must go down to the coffee-maker on the thirteenth floor!" Sinter exclaimed.

"Why doesn't he get his secretary to do it for him?" asked Saker.

"Who cares?" Minh answered. "Maybe he doesn't trust her either. Maybe he's fussy about his coffee. All that matters is he has followed this exact pattern every day this week. That leaves eight minutes for you to get into Amir's office and set things up."

"It'd be much better if I was in there already," reasoned Saker.

"So we need to figure out a way to get you in," said Minh.

"And what about getting out again?" Saker asked.

Sinter had that one covered. "I've got an idea for that. As long as you're not scared of heights."

21

Three a.m.: the time of night when the body is at its lowest ebb, and every human is either fast asleep or wishing they were. A distant dog bark echoed through the empty streets of the marina plaza, and a spiny rat rustled in the edible delights of an upturned dustbin. Down one of the alleys, a shadow flickered and was gone.

Saker padded across the concrete, dancing through the darkness, avoiding the spill of the streetlights. He wore a headset, and carried a small rucksack. Instructions were being relayed all the way from Ho Chi Minh to his earpiece. Minh had a feed from all the security cameras covering the area. They were arranged in a mosaic on his screen. He talked Saker through every move he had to make.

"Stop there. A guard with a dog will pass in front of you in ten, nine, eight . . ."

As he counted down, Saker crouched, trying to make himself invisible.

"Three, two, one."

Right on cue, an armed guard, leading a German shepherd dog, walked along the street.

"Light will sweep in from the left," Minh commentated, "then go!"

Saker sprinted across the gap in front of him, leapt over a low hedge, and squeezed down into the flowerbeds.

"A minute to the next count," Minh reported.

Sinter had commented that day quite how much this whole operation had changed Minh. Beforehand he'd barely spoken a word, he'd been taciturn and withdrawn. It seemed that the mission had given him a challenge, a purpose, a reason for doing what he did. Admittedly he was still awkward and not the kind of person you'd want to be sitting next to on a long bus journey, but he had come alive. And while he still rubbed Saker up the wrong way, his knowledge and skills were quite remarkable.

"Counting to security camera blindspot, in ten, nine, eight . . ."

Then Saker was up and running again, eyes dead ahead on his target, a side entrance to the building. As he arrived in the covered doorway, he heard the tell-tale beeping that warned an alarm was about to go off.

"Minh," he whispered, then with more urgency, "MINH! I think I've tripped an alarm! It's going to go off!"

"Tell me something I don't know," Minh responded.

"What am I going to do?" Saker pressed.

"You're going to shut up and let me deal with it."

Saker sweated as the beeps increased in intensity, pressing himself against the wall – it seemed the alarm would go off at any second. Then without warning, a red light on the door handle flashed to green, and the beeping abruptly stopped.

"What are you waiting for?" Minh asked. "It's open."

The lifts were out of bounds, as they would be alarmed, so Saker had to take the stairs. Up thirty storeys. By the time he reached the penthouse floor, he was breathing heavily, his legs were leaden and most of his adrenalin was long gone. Minh directed him to the grand office in the corner suite, and Saker crept inside. The office was even more plush than he had imagined. The wall was one vast glass screen over the marina, and much of the centre of the room was taken up by an enormous green leather-topped desk.

"Right, well I guess I just need to hole up here till morning then," said Saker into the mic.

"Just don't fall asleep," Minh instructed sternly.

"As if!" said Saker, lying on the thick carpet. "I'm like a coiled spring, ready for action."

It seemed only minutes later that he woke up. Sunlight was streaming through the glass window. Saker yawned, stretched and rubbed the sleep out of his eyes. That carpet was comfy! Then Minh's last words to him rang in his ears. In a sudden panic, he rolled up his sleeve and looked at his watch. It was ten minutes to nine o'clock. Saker leapt to his feet at the exact second that he heard Amir greeting his secretary behind the door. Saker looked around for a hiding spot. There was only one place he could go. He sprinted behind the desk, squeezing into the space where the chair would fit, as Amir walked into the office. Saker could hear him walking up to the desk, heard the sound as he placed his briefcase down, then turned to leave. Saker breathed out. But then stopped in horror. His headset! It was still lying on the carpet in full view, right where Amir would walk. Through a gap under the desk he watched as Amir's hand-stitched leather shoes paced right past the headset, coming millimetres from crunching it. This time he did breathe out, closing his eyes and rubbing his chin in relief.

The door closed. The clock was ticking. Saker squeezed out and grabbed the headset, pulling it on.

"I told you not to fall asleep!" Minh shouted at him. "I've been calling you for nearly an hour. We have eight minutes to make this work."

"Stop shouting at me and tell me what to do!"

Then abruptly the door opened again. Saker slammed himself against the wall behind the door. He held his breath as Amir's secretary went to the desk and carefully placed his newspapers down on the leather. At the last second before she turned around, Saker reached out to the door handle, and pulled it back towards him, covering himself with the open door. The secretary exited. He'd got away with it . . . for now!

"We need to get inside that briefcase," Minh ordered.

Saker picked it up. Like everything else in the office, the briefcase felt expensive.

"Crocodile skin," he noted, and then with dismay, "and a five-number pass code!"

"Write down the numbers on it," Minh said. Saker scribbled them onto the palm of his hand.

"Right, now the majority of people never bother to programme their codes from the factory preset. So try 00000, 11111 and everything up to 99999."

Saker tried every one, as frantically as he could. "No good!"

"12345."

"Nope! Six minutes and counting."

"Right then, try his birthday. 21473."

"No good, Minh – this is never going to work, there are a hundred thousand possibilities here."

"Only if the code is totally random . . . which it never is," replied Minh firmly. "Right, next thing to try: most people when they shut a briefcase simply close it, then give the barrels of the lock one spin. Amir is right-handed, so set the numbers back to where they were, then give one spin with your thumb – he would have gone downwards, so you go upwards. That should reverse the spin."

Saker saw the logic in this, but knew it would never work. He spun the dials. Nothing. He reset the numbers and tried again. Still nothing.

"This is ludicrous," he said, giving it one more spin. "We're going to have to break into this the old-fashioned way . . . oh." There was a click. The latch popped up. "No way! Minh, you're incredible!"

"Five minutes," Minh reminded him. "What have you got?"

"He has a brand new laptop . . . that figures, a card reader for his bank account, some papers, and his wallet."

"Right, give me all the credit card and bank card numbers – no need to read them out, just point the camera at them. Then switch the card reader for the one I gave you. And I need to get a look at all the papers in there. You don't have to hold them for long – I'll take grabs."

Saker spooled through everything as quickly as he could, all the while Minh's voice nagging in his ear, "three minutes . . . two, come on, FASTER!"

"OK, Minh, done. What now?"

"Right, you need to insert the transmitter into the USB socket."

Saker did as he was told. The transmitter was tiny, and sat almost flush with the laptop itself. It was invisible to the casual viewer, but if Amir examined his laptop too closely, or tried to put anything into that USB socket, then they would be busted.

"Nearly done." Saker was pouring sweat.

Finally, the last of them. Saker shut the briefcase, and re-spun the barrels of the lock.

"He's coming back!" Minh practically yelled. Saker could hear him. Amir had come back to the office early!

"Stall him!" Saker hissed. Too late, he could see the door handle twisting. It was all about to come crashing down around them!

"Pak Amir." It was the secretary, calling out to him behind the door. "Could you just sign this contract?" The door handle was released.

A stroke of luck! Saker slammed the briefcase shut. He snapped the camera off his headset, and plugged it to the cabinet with a lump of Blu-Tack, pointing roughly at where Amir would be sitting. Then he dashed to the window, popped the catch and swung the window open. But he'd forgotten something! Reaching into his backpack, he pulled out a note and planted it on the desk on top of Amir's newspapers.

Your actions are destroying the forests the whole planet depends on. We are watching and do not forgive. We are going to take from you everything you value.

It was signed *The Ghosts of the Forest*.

And last, the symbol. This had been Sinter's idea. Carved from precious rainforest wood, it signified both the death and the potential of the forests. The bullet shape had just the right amount of threat. Many soldiers believe there is somewhere a bullet with their name on it. It had taken Saker hours to carve it, and then to brand the image of the falcon's head on the base, right where the firing cap would be on a real bullet. It was simple, but meaningful. He placed the bullet on top of the note.

Saker slipped out of the window, hauling himself into space and pulling the window closed behind him. At that moment Amir opened the door and walked in. Saker's fingertips dug into the gaps where the glass was welded into the building's metal framework, and he swung to face the windows. His toes scrabbled for purchase on the glass; beneath his feet was a hundred metres of empty air. At this height, the wind was rushing and whirling. He had never felt so exposed.

"Saker!" a voice called from above him. He looked up. Sliding towards him was the trolley used to clean the windows of the building, and standing in the middle of it was his friend.

"Climb up!" Sinter called.

"That's easy for you to say!" Saker grumbled back, before grunting with effort as he inched his fingers up the side of the window. His foot slipped on the gripless surface, and his feet flailed over the vast drop. Sinter yelped with fear. Toes back on the metal, Saker carefully made his way, hand over hand, up to the trolley. He gripped hold of the structure like a drowning man grabbing a life-raft, and powered up to safety. Instinctively, he grabbed Sinter in a bear hug, breathing heavily.

"Enough of that," Sinter said, pushing him away. "We're not done yet."

"Yeah, yeah," Saker agreed, pulling his laptop out of his rucksack. Sinter sat next to him with another laptop. They sat on the trolley, feet swinging over the abyss, like two pals on a park bench doing their homework. Sinter's screen showed Minh's face beamed from Ho Chi Minh. Saker's screen showed the feed from the small camera that he'd planted inside Amir's office, and another window, as yet blank. As they watched, Amir sat down at his desk and read the note, then lifted the bullet in his fingers. They saw his secretary come in, and then leave again, and watched as Amir turned the bullet in his hands, obviously wondering what it signified.

"Come on, come on," Saker urged.

"Be patient," Sinter said.

Amir reached for his briefcase and opened it, taking out his laptop, placing it on the desk in front of him. He powered it up. Suddenly the empty window on Saker's laptop came to life. It showed an exact representation of Amir's laptop screen. The transmitter in his USB socket was sending the information directly to them.

"It's working!" Saker's excitement brimmed over.

"It's called 'Wardriving'," explained Minh. "Amir thinks he's using the internet, but he's actually operating a ghost profile through your laptop. As long as you can stay within a few metres of him, we can 'sniff' everything he does. We've got him!"

The pair watched, fascinated, as Amir called up a banking website, and started typing in numbers.

"Zoom the camera in on his fingers," Minh instructed. They did as they were told, and Minh slowed down the images in order to see what he was typing.

"He's gone for his daughter's birthday as his password!" Minh was triumphant. "Some people have no idea about security!"

"No one expects a sneak like you to be watching," Saker murmured.

"OK, I have those details," Minh said. "Now let's hope he goes for the big one."

"Looks like he is," said Saker, as another banking website popped up on screen. This time Amir had to use their credit card machine in order to access the account. What popped up on screen made Saker and Sinter gasp.

"That's over fifty million dollars!" Sinter whispered.

"He's making an absolute fortune," Saker agreed.

"Correction," added Minh. "He *was* making a fortune."

With that, Minh hit a few keys, and the final part of the operation began.

Amir was confused. How on earth had the bullet and note got onto his desk? Of course, it was just another idle threat from some loony green group – nothing to worry about. However, there was something about it that nagged him.

We will take everything you value. He was a careful man; you didn't get to his position without keeping tabs on one's own finances. He fired up his laptop, and went straight to the websites that held his account details. Just as he thought, the first site showed nothing untoward. This was ridiculous. Best to try his second account though. He went through all the security procedures needed to access it – one couldn't be too careful. And there it was: a nice fat figure of tens of millions of dollars, money creamed off all the deals he'd made in selling off Borneo's forests to the highest bidders. He sighed, half with relief, half with smugness, and sat back in his seat.

But then something weird happened. All of a sudden, the arrow of his cursor started to move across the screen all on its own. Amir watched in confusion as the cursor moved to the button marked "Make transfer". It clicked on the box. Amir sat up straight, and moved his fingers on the mousepad. Nothing. Instead the cursor moved to the box asking how much he wanted to transfer. He watched in horror as the cursor clicked "All funds". And then numbers were being entered in the boxes in front of him. He started furiously stabbing at keys, clicking ESCAPE and BACK, but the computer seemed to have a mind of its own. A status bar popped up on screen. It read, "transferring funds", and started growing second by second. In desperation Amir smashed his fist down on the laptop, then picked it up and hurled it against the wall. There was a splintering sound, and the screen sputtered and died.

Up on the trolley, Saker and Sinter held their breath as the status bar crept closer and closer to completion. A mere millimetre from the end, they saw Amir smash the laptop. They'd been so close . . . just seconds from completion and they'd failed! But then, as they looked at the screen, it blinked once, and a message popped up: "Transfer complete." The window returned to the account's homepage. In the box that had read 50,000,000 dollars, there was now just one digit. It was "0". At that second, the screen buzzed and died. From the camera inside the office, they watched as Amir stamped his laptop into smithereens.

Amir walked like a drunk man to his chair, and slumped into it. He made to reach for the phone, then sat back, uncertain. At that second the phone rang, and he jumped as if he had heard a gunshot. Surely they couldn't be calling already? A man in his position may be powerful, but also has a lot of enemies. Some pretty scary people were watching his movements very carefully indeed. He looked at the phone as if it were a viper coiled on his desk. They saw him pick up the phone and answer. As he listened, the big, fat, important man shrank in his chair – a bully thoroughly beaten.

"Time to make our exit," Saker suggested.

22

Late afternoon in the montane forest, the clouds rampaged up deep gullies. Altitude tainted the damp air with chill. For the humans on the forest floor, every outward breath blew steam like a half-boiled kettle. In a glade cut with a single beam of golden sunlight, Sinter sat brushing out the tangles in the black tresses of her hair. Alongside her, an elderly woman stood with eyes closed, singing a haunting refrain. The wrinkles in her face were so deep that she appeared almost mummified, but she had a striking beauty. On the other side of the fire, Saker had a small boy playing in his lap. He was carving a spoon out of a single sliver of wood, showing the child how to shape the timber. The child watched, totally engrossed.

A Penan man appeared alongside him, tapping Saker on the shoulder. "It is time." Saker nodded to his friend across the fire; they stood and followed the diminutive bushman. He led them past temporary shelters where members of their new Clan sat chatting, smoking, preparing food, living their lives. Finally they came to a building, which had clearly been standing much longer than the others. The roof was high, steep and thatched, below it was a small door. Normally it was taboo for a girl to enter this Clan house, but a special exception had been made. Saker and Sinter stooped, stepping into the half-light. A fire in the centre of the room cast leaping shadows up and down the walls. Wooden masks with empty eyes stared down from the walls; warrior forms, their bodies slick with sweat, were sitting around the fire. They were panting after hours of dancing. The couple entered, bowing their heads to the Clan chief, who gestured to them to sit by the fire. The chief was no taller than Saker's chest, but had an undeniable presence. Around his throat he wore a necklace of crocodile teeth, and his hair was cropped in a blunt fringe. He began a chant, stomping his feet and aiming his spear at the young pair in a manner that looked impossibly threatening. Saker and Sinter both knew this was a ritual challenge – to accept it they must hold their ground. In the gloom behind the chief, another figure sat cross-legged, stroking his stubbly chin with one hand, before reaching up to clean his glasses on his shirt. Hagen, they both thought.

The chief began to take on the form of a monitor lizard, tongue flickering as it searched for food. Then he danced like a strutting bird, before becoming a striking pit viper. Finally his limbs became inhumanly loose and limber, hanging down, his eyes cast around him with an ease that seemed to be nonchalant, but which took in everything about him. He scratched his stomach in a manner almost human, but not quite. He had become the man of the forest, the orang utan. As they watched, his movements morphed into the human movements of a Penan warrior and then back again. His dance was simple but significant: the Penan and the orang utan are one, wild men of the forest, bound to the jungle. Humans are not special – we are just primates. Science tells us that mere morsels of our genes are different from those of a chimpanzee, and that we are more closely related to an orang utan than a beetle is to a fly. Somehow the dance told that same truth even more eloquently.

When the dance was done, two Penan were assigned to each of the youngsters. They each took a small wooden bowl of black soot, and dipped into it a sliver of sharp bamboo. Then they started to stab tiny dots in Saker's and Sinter's upper arms. The process was intensely painful, but the pair knew better than to show they were feeling any pain. Gradually the tattoos started to take shape. The form was like a whirlpool, but with two swirls coming together, reminiscent of the Chinese yin and yang symbols. The shape symbolised dark and light, timelessness, the world of their ancestors and of future generations always bound together. It was a mark reserved for those who had proved themselves in the ways of the Penan. When the marks were finished, the ritual was done, and stern faces gave way to huge grins. The pair embraced their new family like brother and sister.

Later, they left with Hagen, and walked a small way off into the forest, away from the singing and dancing that would continue into the early hours.

Hagen spoke. "Amir was taken into prison last night."

Saker and Sinter gasped with elation, and not a little disbelief.

"I never quite allowed myself to believe it could work," said Saker.

"When all the information you captured hit the international press, it was too much for him. And you'd made sure he had no money to fall back on. He couldn't escape."

"I guess there is some justice," Saker said.

"There'll be even harsher justice for him when he gets out of prison," Hagen continued. "He owes some very powerful people an awful lot of money."

"He'll be replaced," said Sinter glumly.

"Yes, but hopefully the Malaysian government will have learned a lesson," said Hagen, "and it will be a long time before anyone can get that kind of money together again."

They stood in silence for a few minutes, enjoying the sun setting over the trees.

"So what are we going to do with fifty million dollars?" asked Saker.

"Buy a yacht?" joked Sinter.

"An island?" added Saker. "Or just blow it all on one massive party!"

The smiles settled. But what in all seriousness were they going to do with it?

"I guess we can just buy the Penan's forest and give it to them . . ." Sinter suggested.

". . . and create a massive national park where orang utans can be protected," Saker continued.

". . . and buy a lot of global publicity," Sinter finished. Now they were completing each other's sentences!

Hagen held up a hand to stop them in their tracks. "I've been thinking," he said. "We don't need all of that money here. And your place is not buried here in the forest. The Penan are not your concern."

They looked at him, aghast. "What do you mean, not our concern? Of course they are! They're family – you can't want to get rid of us? After all we've done?"

Hagen shook his head, removed his glasses and rubbed his eyes. "No." He cleaned his glasses and put them back on again. "You have done more for these people than they or you will ever know. They are now your Clan and you will always be welcome here. But you had a plan. A big plan, and it was bigger than just saving a small part of the forest, much bigger than I could ever dream of."

There was silence. They waited for him to continue.

"There are more problems in this world than those of the Ghosts of the Forest. You have an opportunity to make a real difference. And don't forget, *they* will still be looking for you."

The pair knew that *they* meant the other Clan. The Clan that wanted them silenced.

"*They* will hear about what has happened here and come looking. If you're smart, you'll keep moving. Keep moving, and keep making a difference. There are a million more ghosts that need your help."

EPILOGUE

The six o'clock cicada is in full voice, a penetrating natural police siren through the green caverns. Frogs ribbit and burp with the closing dusk. The mist grows and fades like windblown steam through the canopy. Four hornbills take flight, and sweep their vast wings, flying in fighter-jet formation over the valley beneath them. A Brahminy kite, chocolate above and ivory beneath, circles on stiff, broad wings, carried effortlessly aloft by rising warm air currents. Far below, Sinter prods the embers of a fire, the eye-stinging smoke keeping the biting bugs at bay.

Underneath a simple banana-leaf lean-to, Sinter and Saker huddle next to each other, sheltered from the pelting rain that hammers into the leaves about them. For the first time in weeks, they open up the laptop that has served them so well. They have set a portable satellite dish high in the forest canopy to get a good view of the sky. Even so, the internet signal is intermittent and poor, so they've not bothered to use it since they've been back in the jungle. Slowly, the computer connects. Not surprisingly, the email inbox does not fill with messages. In fact there is only one. It is from Minh. Clicking on it, a series of photos pop up on screen. The first is a map, of a remote peninsula within the Arctic circle in Siberia. Next is a photo that makes both of them gasp. It is a heavy-set black wolf, its eyes piercing amber, exquisitely beautiful and majestic. Then images of the landscapes, trees sparkling with windblown frost, snow-crusted mountains, great frozen wildernesses. Abruptly these are replaced by images of huge oil refineries, chugging black smoke into the icy sky. And then finally, one image that would live long in their minds: a line of fur coats hanging on the wall of a building. Except they are not fur coats. They are dead wolves, hanging by their tails. Alongside them, a hunter, ruddy-faced, rifle in one hand, bottle of some dirty spirit in the other, grinning with delight at what he's achieved. Saker and Sinter look at each other, knowing exactly what is being asked of them.

"Well, I guess we'd better not get too used to the tropics. I've had enough of humidity anyhow." the boy jokes.

"Yup . . . it looks like we're going to need some nice woolly jumpers," the girl replies.

With that, Saker closes the laptop, and takes his pocket knife out. In his left hand is a fine piece of ironwood, no longer than a thumb. Saker begins the long process of whittling it down, into the shape of a bullet.

AUTHOR'S NOTE

This book is a mix of real life and fiction. The Penan and Iban are real, though their lifestyles are fading fast. My descriptions are taken from diaries of my many expeditions to Borneo, a place I love dearly. Saker's cave is based on the vast sinkhole "Solo", in the Mulu mountains of Sarawak in Borneo. For a BBC series, caving legend Tim Fogg, camerawoman Justine Evans and I were the first to explore the caverns that ran for an eternity beneath the mighty sinkhole. It was a place that chilled and thrilled me in equal measure. Trying to wriggle through a tiny squeeze in a boulder choke, I got stuck in one of the tunnels. Tim told me we'd have to leave me there for a few days until I lost enough weight to struggle free! That was the beginning of a claustrophobia I suffer from to this day, the fear that Saker suffers from is very much taken from my own experience!

When I first visited Borneo in the early 1990s, if you

looked down from a plane or helicopter all you could see in every direction was jungle. Now, there is very little left. Instead, it's just oil palm plantations stretching out to the horizon.

Down at ground level, the jungle is always alive with sounds from frogs, insects, birds and monkeys. The plantations though are as silent as the grave.

The character of Amir and his illegal activities are entirely fictional. However, it is entirely true that Malaysia has in recent times had senior politicians in control of both logging and the environment, responsible for both cutting the forests down and for protecting them. It is also true that Southeast Asia is suffering more rapid deforestation than the Amazon rainforest, and most of Borneo's rainforest will be gone within a decade. Mass burning of the jungle has led to summers where the whole of Southeast Asia has been clouded in poisonous smog, with people barely able to see or breathe. Animals such as the orang utan are being squeezed into ever decreasing sanctuaries.

Lars Hagen is based on the real life Bruno Manser. His Herculean efforts to protect the Penan are true. He is the kind of person I wish I could be: someone who gave up everything to make a real difference to the world. Sadly, it is a fiction that he still lives in the forest, pulling the strings and helping the Penan. There have been no sightings of him since the early years of the twenty-first century. I hope that his family and friends will see this book as a tribute to someone whose legacy I hold in the highest regard.

The character of Roisin is based on a real Irish philanthropist I met working in Vietnam. The tunnels of the Viet Cong, and the situation with landmines and unexploded ordnance in Vietnam, Cambodia and Laos is unfortunately worse than my words could convey.

I hope this book is entertaining first and foremost, but should anyone wish to act on the themes found within, then so much the better. I absolutely do not want people to believe that the situation with world conservation is hopeless. It is imperative that we all know we can make a difference. You don't have to be activists like my fictional heroes to change the world, simply taking in interest in what you buy, what products you use and where they come from, thinking about your own personal impact on the planet... all these things are the very best of starts!

If you want to find out more about the situation with palm oil then there are many resources online, including www.greenpeace.org.uk/forests/palm-oil.

Should you wish to get involved in buying and "retiring" a chunk of rainforest, have a look at schemes such as those found here: www.orangutan.org.uk/, www.rainforest-rescue. org, www.worldlandtrust.org/projects/malaysia and www. rainforestconcern.org.

Steve Backshall
Somewhere on the Baja peninsula, Mexico
November 2012.

Don't miss book 3 of

**THE
FALCON
CHRONICLES**

WILDS OF THE WOLF

coming in 2014.

the orion star

Sign up for **the orion star**
newsletter to get inside information
about your favourite children's authors
as well as exclusive competitions and
early reading copy giveaways.

www.orionbooks.co.uk/newsletters

Follow @the_orionstar on .

Orion
Children's Books